# The Doom of
# the Haunted Opera

# THE DOOM
# OF THE
# HAUNTED OPERA

## JOHN BELLAIRS
Completed by Brad Strickland

*Frontispiece
by Edward Gorey*

*Dial Books for Young Readers
New York*

Published by Dial Books for Young Readers
A Division of Penguin Books USA Inc.
375 Hudson Street
New York, New York 10014

Library of Congress Cataloging in Publication Data
Bellairs, John.
The doom of the haunted opera / John Bellairs
completed by Brad Strickland
frontispiece by Edward Gorey.—1st ed.
p.  cm.
Summary: Lewis Barnavelt and Rose Rita Pottinger are
faced with a dilemma when their discovery of an unpublished
opera score unleashes a wicked sorcerer who plans
to rule the world by bringing back the dead.
ISBN 0-8037-1464-5.—ISBN 0-8037-1465-3 (library)
[1.Wizards—Fiction.  2. Magic—Fiction.
3. Supernatural—Fiction.]  I. Strickland, Brad.  II. Title.
PZ7.B413Do  1995  [Fic]—dc20  94-45798  CIP  AC

Thanks to Jeanne Sharp,
reader and advisor.
—B.S.

*For Ann and Tony LaPietra,*
*who helped me explore the haunted opera!*
B.S.

*The Doom of*
*the Haunted Opera*

# CHAPTER ONE

"Thank you for coming, Florence. Kids, you may as well stay and hear this too," said Jonathan Barnavelt. It was a cold late-winter Saturday morning in the early 1950s. Jonathan looked unusually solemn, although nothing else about him had changed. His red beard was as bushy as ever, and he wore his usual outfit of tan wash pants, blue work shirt, and red vest. He stood behind the desk in his study holding a letter, and it was this letter that had brought them all together in the big old Barnavelt home on High Street in New Zebedee, Michigan.

Gathered in the Barnavelt study were Jonathan's next-door neighbor, Mrs. Florence Zimmermann, his nephew Lewis, and Lewis's best friend, Rose Rita Pottinger. Mrs. Zimmermann was a trim, elderly woman with a disorderly mop of white hair and a friendly, wrinkly-faced smile. She wore a purple sweater, a purple woolen skirt, and purple galoshes. She happened to be a witch, but she was a good magician and not the evil kind.

Mrs. Zimmermann was also a fabulous cook, and she had been making a blueberry pie when Lewis ran over to ask her to join them. Now she sat in a straight chair, with a puzzled expression on her face and a white smudge of flour beside her nose. Lewis, a stocky, blond boy of about thirteen, stood behind her. Beside him was Rose Rita, who was almost a year older than Lewis but in the same class at school. Outside the study a blustery March wind rattled the bare black trees and swept dustings of snow off the rooftops. A dark gray sky threatened more snow or sleet, but so far today there had just been stormy gusts of wind. "All right, Weird Beard," Mrs. Zimmermann said in a teasing voice. "Stop being so formal. Tell us about this mysterious message you've received."

Uncle Jonathan sighed. He unfolded the letter, a sheet of thick, official-looking paper the buttery color of cream, and said, "I suppose you remember Lucius Mickleberry."

Lewis and Rose Rita just looked at each other blankly. The odd name meant nothing to them. Mrs. Zimmermann chuckled. "Of course I remember him—probably better than you do," she said. Mrs. Zimmermann explained to Lewis and Rose Rita. "Lucius was New Zebedee's leading sorcerer, at least until he retired just after the war."

"He moved to Florida in 1947," said Jonathan.

With a smile Mrs. Zimmermann asked, "How is the dear old coot?"

Jonathan gave her a sorrowful look. "Maybe I'd better read the letter to you," he said. He sat down and turned on the old-fashioned lamp with its pewter base and milk-glass dome. Soft light spilled across the top of the desk, making the room somehow feel a little warmer. Jonathan put on his brown tortoise-shell reading glasses, coughed to clear his throat, and began to read aloud:

> *Dear Jonathan,*
> *If you have received this letter, then I am dead.*
> *Before you read one more line, go and get Florence*
> *Zimmermann, because she should be in on this too.*

"Oh," said Mrs. Zimmermann, looking upset. "Lucius is dead? I had no idea he was even ailing. What else does it say?"

Jonathan looked up, irritation showing in his face. "How should I know, Frizzy Wig?" he asked impatiently. "I did just what the letter said and sent for you before I read one more line."

"Well, read it all, Brush Mush. Time's a-wasting," said Mrs. Zimmermann. Although her words were as sharp as ever, Lewis noticed that her voice sounded a little tearful. She took a tissue out of her sweater pocket and wiped her eyes as she sniffled.

Jonathan himself looked weepy-eyed. Clearing his throat again, he read aloud:

*Now, please don't feel sorry for me, you two. I have lived a good long time and have had a full life. In fact, the last few years have been dreary. Age has slowed me down and has made me weak and shaky. To tell the truth, I am looking forward to the Other Side. I have a clear conscience, so I hope it will be to my liking.*

*On to business. You may know that I have a granddaughter down here in St. Petersburg. She has married a respectable, perfectly ordinary man, and she has no idea that her old granddad is a wizard. That's where you come in. I have named you, Jonathan, the executor of my estate. Your job is to distribute my property after my death. I am willing all my magical books to you, because you'll know what to do with them. You'll have to travel down here to St. Petersburg to do your job, but my estate will pay for the trip, so look on it as a free vacation.*

*There is one other job to do: I have a collection of amulets and talismans. Some of them are pretty powerful stuff, and some are so evil that they must remain for safekeeping in the hands of a good magician. Since Florence Zimmermann (Hi, Florence. Do you still love purple?) is the best judge I know of such trinkets, please persuade her to come along. The estate will take care of her traveling expenses too, and there is also a small bequest for both of you. I've enclosed my lawyer's card. He will see that you get this letter when I am gone, and he will have further instructions for you. Please give him a telephone call, and he will work out all the details.*

*That is about all. If I miss anything in the Other World, it will be the friendship of people like you. Think of me now and then and always remember me as your friend.*

Lucius Mickleberry

Uncle Jonathan finished reading the letter, folded it, and laid it on his desk. Then he fished a red bandanna from his pocket and blew his nose with a loud honk. "That's it," he said. "I have the lawyer's card. Should we call?"

"I suppose so," Mrs. Zimmermann said. She sighed. "Well, God rest Lucius's soul. He was a good friend, and I will really miss him."

"Who was he?" asked Rose Rita.

Jonathan smiled in a sad, reminiscent way. "For one thing, he was the president of the Capharnaum County Magicians Society for about thirty years," he said. "He was a wizard who could do lots of magic, mostly with the weather. And above all else, he was a good man. When I was still a youngster, Lucius dealt with some pretty nasty sorcery right here in New Zebedee. No one ever found out what he had done—no one except his fellow magicians, that is. It was typical of Lucius that he never claimed any reward or glory for saving the whole town from an awful fate. But that's a long story, and I'll tell you about it some other time."

"Uncle Jonathan," said Lewis suddenly, "are there witches and warlocks and sorcerers *everywhere?*"

Mrs. Zimmermann and Jonathan Barnavelt exchanged

an amused look. Then Jonathan said, "Well, more in some places than in others. Haggy Face, do you want to explain? You're the real McCoy here. I'm just a parlor magician."

Mrs. Zimmermann wiped her eyes one last time. Then she touched her chin with her finger and said, "Well, you see, Lewis, magic is a bit like gold or silver. It doesn't exist just anywhere. There are places that have veins of magic running through them, just as you find some locations with veins of gold or silver ore. In the United States, there are, oh, maybe a dozen or so places where magic flows more strongly than elsewhere. It just so happens that one of the strongest magic lodes of all is right here in New Zebedee, Michigan, believe it or not."

"That sounds a little funny, Mrs. Zimmermann. I mean, you don't really *mine* magic," objected Rose Rita. She looked very serious in her long black hair and heavy black-rimmed glasses, and she was a levelheaded, logical girl.

"No," agreed Mrs. Zimmermann, with a laugh. "You don't exactly go after it with picks and shovels, but the magical power is here, in the air, so to speak. Oh, don't get me wrong. A true magician can work his enchantment just about anywhere, but he will do much better when there is a strong current of magic flowing all around to call upon. Then the spells are a lot more powerful and a lot more effective. Of course, some people are more naturally talented at magic than others—"

"Hey, watch it, Pruny Face," growled Jonathan in

mock anger. "Just because you can do real magic and I'm pretty much stuck with creating illusions—"

"Present company excepted, Brush Mush," replied Mrs. Zimmermann before continuing. "Anyway, some people, like Lucius, could become very powerful magicians here in New Zebedee, while others, like poor old Mildred Jaeger, could never get a spell right to save their lives. Still, in a focus of power like New Zebedee even Mildred could work a little magic, even if it didn't do exactly what she intended. That is why so many wizards and sorcerers and thaumaturgists gravitate to this town. And that is why people like Lucius Mickleberry's father began the Capharnaum County Magicians Society more than a hundred years ago. You see, if good magicians can draw on the power, then so can evil ones. So we members of the society are sort of an honor guard. We keep the mystical operations safe and on the level, and we prevent any evil sorcerer from taking advantage of New Zebedee's magical currents."

"And in the meantime," put in Jonathan, "we have meetings and play cards and swap lies about how great we are. So it works out quite well all around. We can protect the earth from evil wizardry, and at the same time we can get in a few games of penny-ante poker and munch on Haggy's delicious fudge brownies."

"Thank you for the compliment, Frazzle Face," said Mrs. Zimmermann with a smile. Then in a quieter voice she asked, "When are you going to call the lawyer?"

"Well, it's Saturday, but this card has the lawyer's home telephone number. No time like the present," Jonathan said as he reached for the phone. After several minutes Jonathan hung up and heaved a great sigh. "Well, Haggy," he said, "the lawyers acted really fast in mailing me that letter. There will be a memorial service for Lucius the day after tomorrow, and I'd like to attend, if possible."

"Yes," Mrs. Zimmermann said. "So would I."

"In that case, we'll have to fly down," Jonathan said.

Mrs. Zimmermann made a face. Even though she was a witch, she hated the idea of flying. "All right," she said in a resigned voice. "Make the arrangements. I'll drive us to the airport, though. I don't trust that antique clunker of yours to get us there—or your driving either, for that matter."

"What about me?" Lewis asked in a small voice. "Am I going too?"

His uncle smiled sympathetically. "I think not, Lewis. This job may take a couple of weeks, and you can't miss that much school."

"He can stay at my house," Rose Rita volunteered at once.

"That's very generous of you, Rose Rita," Jonathan replied. "However, your mother and dad might not feel very comfortable with that arrangement. I don't like un-invited guests myself, and I wouldn't palm one off on your folks. Actually, there shouldn't be a problem. Mrs. Holtz will probably be glad to stay here in the house and keep an eye on everything." Hannah Holtz was a short, apple-cheeked woman who came in twice a week to help with the housework. She was cheerful, chirpy, and she let Lewis do pretty much anything that didn't threaten to destroy the house. Like many others in New Zebedee, Mrs. Holtz knew that Jonathan was some kind of magician, although she would have been astonished to learn that he did his tricks with real magic and not with mirrors or with gimmicks concealed in his sleeves. She had stayed with Lewis once before, when Jonathan had business in the Upper Peninsula for a few days. "I'll call her," Jonathan said, "if that's all right, Lewis."

Lewis smiled. That was one of the many reasons he liked living with his uncle. Jonathan never treated him as if he were a child. "Sure," he said. "That will be fine. Now Rose Rita won't have to find a new partner for our project."

Mrs. Zimmermann raised her eyebrows. "Oh? Are you two working on some mysterious experiment? What are you doing, building a rocket to the moon?"

Rose Rita grimaced. "Not really. We have this boring assignment to write a report on some local historical place, person, or event. And the other teams have already taken all the good stuff."

Jonathan's eyes twinkled. "You mean like the Civil War heroes, and New Zebedee's World War One flying ace Jimmy Margate, and the bombsight factory that was here during World War Two?" He knew Rose Rita's favorite subjects quite well.

"And even the time that New Zebedee almost became the state capital," she added. "So we're trying to find something that's halfway interesting to work on."

"Well," said Jonathan, "I wish I could help, but I've got to get busy making arrangements."

"That's okay," said Rose Rita with a smile. "We'll think of something."

Mrs. Zimmermann got out of her chair. "I'll be running along. My pie is not about to bake itself. Good luck, you two. We'll think about you down in sunny Florida."

The wind howled outside, and a spatter of sleet clattered against the French windows. It sounded so cold and threatening that Lewis shivered. "Don't rub it in," he said.

# CHAPTER TWO

Jonathan made the arrangements, and that same afternoon he and Mrs. Zimmermann set off in Mrs. Zimmermann's bright purple 1950 Plymouth Cranbrook named Bessie. Mrs. Holtz moved into the guest room in the Barnavelt house on High Street, clucking and tutting about poor Mr. Mickleberry, whom she did not even know. Lewis supposed that Mrs. Holtz sympathized just on general principles.

By Monday afternoon Lewis and Rose Rita had yet to come up with something that might be worth researching. As they sat on the sofa with their notebooks on their laps, Lewis remembered that his uncle had once mentioned a forgotten theater right in the heart of New Zebedee. All the shops on Main Street were old and elaborately decorated, and most of them were two-storied. A few had small businesses like a photographer's studio, an insurance broker, or an employment agency on the second floor. However, the building that housed the five-and-dime and the Farmers' Feed & Seed Company was different. It was taller than all the other establishments on Main Street and took up half a block. And on the top two floors, Jonathan had once remarked, was the New Zebedee Opera House, which had been closed for ages. Lewis suggested this to Rose Rita as a topic they could research.

"Hmm," mused Rose Rita, "I don't know. That sounds pretty dull to me." Her idea of an exciting topic was something that had to do with cannons and cavalry charges.

"Well," Lewis said, ready with the clincher to his argument, "Uncle Jonathan told me that your grandfather designed and built the theater. So what do you think now?"

Rose Rita grinned. Her grandfather on her mother's side was almost ninety years old, but he was active and smart, and she liked him immensely. Grandfather Albert Galway had been many things in his life: a surveyor, a sailor, an architect, and a building contractor, among others. Now he was retired and lived an independent life in a small cottage over on Sycamore Street. "No kidding?" asked Rose Rita. "He never told me that. Okay, Lewis, you're on. What's our first step?"

Lewis was ready for that. "We can interview your grandfather. But I think before we do that, we should try to get a look at the theater. Want to go into town?"

Rose Rita made a face. "It's *freezing* out there."

"It isn't like we're going to the moon, you know," said Lewis with a touch of exasperation. "We can bundle up, and if we hurry, we can be there in ten minutes. Come on, what do you say?"

Rose Rita looked at her watch. It was a quarter to four. "All right," she said with a sigh. "But if I catch pneumonia and die, I'm going to come back as a ghost and haunt you."

Lewis asked Mrs. Holtz for permission to go into town, and she gave it at once, as he knew she would. She was a kind and sweet old lady, but she had about a zillion grandchildren of her own, and she liked to be alone occasionally. Rose Rita and Lewis got into their coats and went outside. It was no longer sleeting, but the wind blew sharp and cold in their faces. They hurried down High Street toward town, their breath coming in frosty puffs and their eyes squinted against the frigid winter air.

The Farmers' Seed & Feed was a cavernous store that smelled of corn and leather and onions. Bins and barrels of seeds cluttered the floor space, while harnesses, bridles, and farm tools hung on the walls. Mr. Pfeiffer owned the feed store and the five-and-dime next door. He was a portly man with a bald head, a fringe of salt-and-pepper hair, and a big red nose that he kept squeezing, as if testing it for ripeness. Lewis and Rose Rita found him sitting in a straight-backed chair next to the store's black potbellied stove, talking to a couple of his customers. The men had settled down for a long conversation, and Mr. Pfeiffer did not look as if he were about to get up.

Lewis explained what he and Rose Rita wanted, and Mr. Pfeiffer squeezed his nose. "Why, sure," he said. "I s'pose it wouldn't hurt for the two of you to have a look around up there. But it'll be awful cold. Tell you what —take a couple of flashlights with you. Get 'em from the shelf there. The electricity's switched off upstairs, and I don't feel like climbing halfway up them stairs just to turn it on." He fumbled in his trouser pocket and found the key to the opera house. "Mind you lock up before you come back down here," he warned them.

With the flashlights in hand, Lewis and Rose Rita went outside, around the corner to Eagle Street, and up the dark flight of stairs that led to the old opera house. Rose Rita turned the key in the lock, and the weathered gray door swung open, groaning on its rusty hinges. Something about the sound made the hair prickle on the back of Lewis's neck, and he clenched his teeth.

He followed Rose Rita into a dim vestibule. Tall, narrow windows gave a little light, but they were cobwebby and dusty, and the cloudy day did little to brighten the place. A thick carpet was underfoot, but Lewis could not tell the color because of a heavy layer of gray dust that covered it. To their left was a counter and a ticket booth. "That must be where the ladies checked their furs," said Rose Rita, flashing her light at the counter. "And where the gentlemen left their overcoats and top hats."

"Oh, sure," said Lewis sarcastically. "I don't think anybody in New Zebedee even *owns* a top hat."

"Well, they used to," insisted Rose Rita. "Look, there are two doorways into the theater. Which one do you want to take?"

"The closest one," replied Lewis. "This dust is going to make me start sneezing in about half a minute."

"It was your idea to come here," Rose Rita reminded him. They padded across the dusty carpet, raising a little mildew-scented cloud as they went toward a wide archway that yawned into the darkness. Just a little farther away was an identical opening, which also led into the auditorium.

Once they had stepped into the theater, Lewis switched on his flashlight too. There were no windows to shed any light in this place, and the faint glow from the vestibule died a few feet inside the doorways. Lewis whistled. "It's bigger than I thought," he said, shining his light this way and that.

Row after row of seats stretched before them, divided into three different-size sections: narrow and wedge-shaped to the right and left sides, and a much wider one down the middle. Two broad, carpeted aisles ran down toward the stage. The seats were covered in plush red velvet, although dust and cobwebs had dulled their luster, and the frames were made of intricate curlicues and loops of wrought iron. The auditorium sloped gently downward from the rear to the front, so the back seats were somewhat higher than the ones closer to the stage. Overhead, in a horseshoe-shaped balcony, benches were arranged like church pews. "How many seats do you suppose?" asked Rose Rita.

"About a thousand," responded Lewis.

Rose Rita snorted. "There aren't that many people in New Zebedee who would *go* to an opera," she said. "Let's count."

Lewis's teeth chattered. It was cold in the dark theater, and he could see his breath in the beam of his flashlight. "I don't want to waste that much time," he said.

Rose Rita sounded amused. "Look, genius, we don't have to count every single seat. All we have to do is count one row from each section and then multiply by the number of rows. You know Miss Fogarty's always complaining that our compositions aren't detailed enough."

"Some details are pretty stupid," muttered Lewis, but just to avoid arguing, he agreed to help Rose Rita count the seats. As they neared the stage, they determined that the theater could hold 480 people, with room for maybe 120 more in the balcony. Lewis turned his flashlight toward the stage. Curtained arches opened on either side, with knee-high railings. The walls were a faded pink, with intricate designs in yellow and red framing the stage. In an oval to the left was the laughing mask of comedy, and to the right of the stage the grieving mask of tragedy, both done in faded gold.

Lewis and Rose Rita came up to the very front. They leaned over the orchestra pit and shined their lights down on rusty music stands, an ancient banged-up grand piano, and a scattering of yellowed, mouse-chewed pages of sheet music.

"Here's the way up to the stage," said Rose Rita. She climbed a few steps and walked to the middle of the stage. There she turned her flashlight on her face and struck a theatrical pose. "O Romeo, Romeo! Wherefore art thou Romeo?" she exclaimed dramatically.

With the flashlight in his hand, Lewis could not clap properly, so he slapped his leg a few times, like someone grudgingly applauding a very poor performer. "Now do the 'Dance of the Seven Veils,' " he cried.

Rose Rita stuck her tongue out at him. "There's a curtain up here with ropes to work it," she said. "I'm going to check out the backstage. Maybe there are dressing rooms or a prop room with swords and armor and stuff."

Lewis had found his way down into the orchestra pit. "Okay," he said. "I'll poke around out here."

The stage creaked faintly as Rose Rita walked away. Now that he was alone, Lewis began to feel a bit uneasy. The darkness seemed to close in all around him, and the cone of light from his flashlight appeared faint and feeble. Lewis began to breathe faster. He was not by nature a brave boy, and he was always imagining all sorts of terrible things that might happen to him. Right now, for instance. He could run into a big, desperate rat in the orchestra pit, or maybe a nest of poisonous snakes that had crept in to spend the winter. Or he might blunder into a creepy web full of venomous spiders—there were certainly enough cobwebs dangling and swaying all over the place. Or—

Oh, get a grip, he told himself. He felt like climbing up out of the pit and finding Rose Rita, but she would know he had scared himself, and she probably would laugh at him. He hated when she did that. So he clenched his teeth and flashed his light over the discolored, uneven keys of the old piano. A wobbly-looking stool sat in front of it, its seat tilted to one side and covered with fuzzy dust. Lewis walked over to the instrument and used one finger to pick out a tune. He hummed to himself as he plunked out the notes of a catchy radio commercial:

> *Pepsi-Cola hits the spot,*
> *Twelve full ounces, that's a lot,*
> *Twice as much for a nickel, too,*
> *Pepsi-Cola is the drink for you.*

Clunk! The last note was a real clinker, dull and flat and unmusical. Lewis frowned and tapped more keys on the bass side of the keyboard. Several in a row made the same thunky noise. It sounded as if something were inside the piano, blocking the strings. Lewis went around to the side and raised the lid, then cast his light into the piano's interior.

No wonder the notes wouldn't play. On the strings lay a thick sheaf of papers, curled at the edges and sallow in the gleam of Lewis's flashlight. He reached for the papers and held them up. They felt brittle and flaky, like crumbling autumn leaves. Because the papers had been inside the piano, little dust had collected on them, and

Lewis could read something written on the cover sheet in a spidery, old-fashioned handwriting:

*The Day of Doom*
———————————
*An Opera in English*
*By Immanuel Vanderhelm*

Lewis heard Rose Rita behind him. "Hey," he said, "look at what I found. This must be really old—"

He looked around and felt a sudden chill. The person standing next to him was not Rose Rita. It was a tall, thin man wearing a long black coat with fur lapels. An outmoded high collar came up to his chin, and the black cravat around his neck glittered with a flashing diamond stickpin. His gray hair was parted in the center, and gray muttonchop whiskers furred his bony cheeks. His horrible eyes were deeply set and staring, like cloudy blue-white marbles with no iris or pupil showing at all. His skin was a ghastly color, sickly white like the belly of a frog. The man's gaping mouth revealed wrinkled black gums and long, snaggly teeth as yellow as the aged ivory keys of the piano. He looked like someone who had been dead for about a month.

"Beware!" the man whispered in a hoarse croak. "Beware the doom of the haunted opera! He means to be King of the Dead!"

Lewis felt frozen to the bone. The man was not standing on the floor but rather floating in the air, and Lewis could tell that his body was not solid but transparent.

The flashlight's beam penetrated him, and Lewis could see the edge of the stage right through the stranger's thin chest. "Beware!" the man groaned again. Then with a horrible moan, the figure became a wisp of vapor and vanished like a dissolving puff of steam. For a second Lewis could only stare, paralyzed with shock.

Then he screamed as loudly as he could.

# CHAPTER THREE

Clutching the sheet music to his chest with his left hand, holding the flashlight in his right, Lewis scrambled out of the orchestra pit and fled toward the dim archway at the back of the auditorium. His running footsteps echoed, and he thought he heard the ghost right behind him. He was almost at the door when something grabbed his coat and yanked him backward. He screeched in terror.

"Hey!" yelled Rose Rita. "Cut it out, Lewis, it's only me."

Lewis almost collapsed with relief. He wouldn't stay in the auditorium, so the two of them went out into the vestibule, where Lewis stood next to one of the dirty windows as if ready to leap out. Then, still panting for breath, he tried to tell Rose Rita what he had seen and heard.

She gave him a doubtful look. "A ghost?" she asked. "Are you sure?"

Lewis nodded. "He looked horrible," he said. "All gray and stiff, and he was as skinny as a board."

Rose Rita sighed. "Lewis, you know what an imagination you have."

Lewis glared at her. "I didn't imagine it," he insisted. "I saw him and I heard him. For Pete's sake, Rose Rita, you've seen some pretty strange things too!" Lewis knew he had a good point. Since she had become friends with Lewis, Rose Rita had witnessed some amazing magical events, both benign and terrifying. Now she looked a little uncertain.

"That's true," admitted Rose Rita with obvious reluctance. "But all of that happened at, well, spooky times and in spooky places. Not in the middle of an ordinary afternoon right in the center of New Zebedee."

"You think *this* isn't a spooky place?" asked Lewis. "It's big and dark and empty, and anything could be in there!"

"I didn't see anything scary," said Rose Rita. "Just the old dressing rooms. And half of them are stuffed with junk from the Seed & Feed and boxes of Mounds and Almond Joys from the five-and-dime. I guess Mr. Pfeiffer uses the back rooms as a warehouse or something. What do you have there?"

Lewis was still gripping the musical score tightly

against his chest. He held it out and said, "I found this hidden inside the piano."

"Hidden, huh?" Rose Rita took the stack of dried-up paper and carefully looked through it. "Seems to be all handwritten. There's music and lyrics and everything. Say, do you know who would love to see this?"

"Who?" Lewis asked.

"Miss White."

Miss White was the music teacher at the junior high school. She was always organizing recitals and performances, and she was always trying to interest her students in fine music. Miss White didn't have much use for the kind of music most young people listened to. She called it bebop and jitterbugging, and with a sniff she would say, "*Truly* educated people have better taste than jitterbugs."

Lewis looked at the sheet music doubtfully. "I don't know," he said slowly. "That's what I was holding when I saw the ghost. Maybe they're connected."

"Okay," responded Rose Rita. She held the sheaf of papers out to him. "Here you are. Just take this back and leave it where you found it. I'll wait here, and we'll just forget that you ever looked inside that piano."

If looks could kill, Lewis's glower would have wiped out half of New Zebedee. "Not me. If you want to hang onto that, it's yours. I'm not going back in there, at least not as long as the electricity's off and there's no light." Lewis had added the last part because he really hated being a coward, and Rose Rita was right about his overactive imagination. He read voraciously, and everything he read lived on very strongly in his imagination. Other kids might be afraid of movie monsters or of spooky radio shows like *Lights Out*, but Lewis populated his own nightmares with terrifying figures like Professor Moriarty, the insidious Dr. Fu-Manchu, the evil Mr. Hyde, and other characters from books.

For a few minutes the two friends stood quietly while Lewis got his breath back. Then, after Rose Rita had carefully locked the door, they went downstairs and gave the flashlights and key back to Mr. Pfeiffer, who was dozing in his chair near the stove while his friends droned on and on to each other about the weather. Once outside Lewis said, "Where to now?"

"Let's go see Grampa Galway," replied Rose Rita. "He can tell us when the opera house was built, and maybe he even knows something about your ghost."

Lewis didn't like the idea very much. "I don't know," he said slowly. "I don't mind talking about stuff like that with Uncle Jonathan and Mrs. Zimmermann, because they understand apparitions and all. But your grandfather might think I'm loony."

"Okay," Rose Rita said. "So we won't tell him about the ghost. Maybe there's another way to find out something about him. Anyway, let's get moving, or I'm going to turn into an icicle."

It was after five, and the day was getting even colder. They walked down Main Street toward the fountain, which the city fathers turned off when the temperature dropped below freezing. The marble columns surrounding it looked as if they had been carved from blocks of polar ice. Rose Rita took the lead, turning left onto Sycamore Street near the drugstore.

Rose Rita's grandfather lived at number 122, in a small one-story cottage. Mr. Galway liked to tinker and build things, and his front yard was crowded with a fish pond (frozen over now), a stone terrace with lawn furniture, and a bench swing hanging from a wooden frame. Lewis had visited here before, and he knew that the backyard was even more cluttered, with about a dozen odd little hand-carved windmills that did crazy things. One was a wooden juggler who tossed four balls in an endless circle. A little old man frantically tried to chop the head off a turkey, but the gobbler always yanked his neck back just in time. A sailing ship swung this way and that in the wind, while the miniature crew frantically moved their arms as if hauling on ropes. Lewis thought the commotion was exciting and fascinating, although Mr. Galway's neighbors had been known to complain that it was all a nuisance.

Rose Rita jumped up to the low front porch, with Lewis right behind her. There was an antiquated twist-type doorbell in the shape of a dog's head with a bone in its mouth. When you grabbed the bone and turned the whole head, the bell made a growling sound. After a few moments Mr. Galway opened the door. He was a tall man with a bald head and bright blue eyes that glittered from behind rimless spectacles. "Well, well," he said genially. "My favorite granddaughter and the Sherlock Holmes expert. Caught any crooks lately, Lewis?"

"Nope," said Lewis with a grin. One of the things Lewis liked most about Mr. Galway was that in his younger days the old man had once attended a lecture on spiritualism by Sir Arthur Conan Doyle, and after the lecture he had shaken hands with the famous author. Lewis had shaken hands with Mr. Galway, so it was almost like he himself had touched the writer of the Sherlock Holmes tales.

"Come in, come in, and don't stand here freezing to death," Mr. Galway said. They went into his living room, which was toasty, and Rose Rita's glasses immediately fogged up. She took them off and polished them with a handkerchief from her coat pocket. The room was crowded but comfortable, with dozens of framed photographs on the wall, a large overstuffed armchair, a long sofa decorated with a Navajo blanket, a magazine rack full of *Popular Mechanics* and *The Saturday Evening Post*, and lots of knickknacks.

Lewis sniffed. The warm air was heavy with delicious aromas of roast beef and cherry pie. Mr. Galway had been a cook in the Navy, and he still prepared all his own meals. "Sit down, you two," said Mr. Galway. "Let me see about a couple of things in the kitchen and I'll be right out."

As Lewis had anticipated, when Mr. Galway returned, he brought back what he called a little snack. It consisted of hot roast-beef sandwiches, tall glasses of milk, and a slice of fresh cherry pie for each of them. They all dug in as Rose Rita told her grandfather what she and Lewis were doing for their history project. She asked him to tell them about the old theater.

"Hmm," mused Mr. Galway. "I remember that, all right. Must have been back about 1900. It was after I worked on the Civil War Memorial, anyway. At first all that space over the Seed & Feed was just empty. It was supposed to be a warehouse or something, but it wasn't well designed for that. Too much trouble to get farm supplies up and down stairs, for one thing. Well, anyway, the New Zebedee Eleemosynary and Cultural League decided there ought to be an auditorium somewhere in town, and they leased that space from old Mr. Pfeiffer, the father of the fellow who runs the store now. They hired me to design the theater, and so I did. Took about two years to build, and she opened in May of 1902. Gilbert and Sullivan's *The Pirates of Penzance*, I remember. I took my wife—my first wife, Coral, rest her soul, not your grandmother, Rose Rita—to the performance."

"When did the theater close?" Rose Rita asked.

Mr. Galway sniffed. "It was after the First World War. I suppose it was about 1919. I'm afraid it never was a big success. Oh, it had its moments. Caruso once gave a concert there, you know, and I remember a great evening when the magician and escape artist Harry Houdini did some amazing things. But most of the time the performances were pretty poorly attended. Then too there was a big influenza epidemic right after the war, and that may have had something to do with it. Of course, that isn't what everyone in town will tell you. They'll say it was because of old Immanuel Vanderhelm and his bad luck."

Lewis glanced at Rose Rita. Immanuel Vanderhelm was the name on the cover of the sheet music he had found inside the piano. "Uh, who was he?" Lewis asked.

"Famous man in his time," said Mr. Galway. "Or at least, that's what I understand. They said he had sung in operas all over the world—Germany, Italy, England, everywhere. And he came to New Zebedee to settle down and retire, but you know how it is. He was like an old fire horse, I guess, always ready to run when he heard a bell."

"What do you mean?" Rose Rita asked as she finished the last bite of her pie.

The old man smiled. "I mean he was always ready to sing or play music or get involved with opera again. Anyway, he wrote a show especially for the theater. Picked out people to be in it and all, rehearsed it, and was supposed to put it on. But then the bad luck started."

Rose Rita leaned forward. "What sort of bad luck do you mean?"

"Well, various problems. His soprano broke her leg and had to be replaced. Then the building where they were making the sets caught fire and burned to the ground. Then the manager of the theater up and disappeared. On top of that, half the people in town were sick with the flu. Then the most mysterious thing of all happened. Opening night came, and Mr. Vanderhelm just didn't show. Left them in the lurch, and I hear tell he might have taken all the box-office money with him too. Anyway, he never returned, and the people in town were so disgusted that they not only cancelled the show, they just locked the theater, even though the League had taken out a ninety-nine-year lease on the space." Mr. Galway pushed himself out of his chair and collected all the dirty dishes on a tray. "Here, now that I think about it, I might be able to dig up something else about that old theater," he said. "You swabs do these dishes for me, and I'll see what I can find."

They went into the kitchen, where Rose Rita washed the dishes and Lewis dried and put them away. By the time they finished and returned to the living room, Mr. Galway had brought a worn, leather-bound family album from his bedroom. He sat on the sofa as he leafed through it, with Lewis on one side and Rose Rita on the other. There were hundreds of photos inside, most of them faded to a brownish tint. Many were of places he had visited while he was in the Navy: Singapore, London, Honolulu, and other exotic ports. Then he stopped and said, "Here it is. This was taken on the opening day of the theater, back in 1902."

Lewis looked. The photo showed about a dozen people standing in the vestibule of the theater, and in the picture everything looked fresh and new. A big poster on the wall behind the group showed a funny-looking man in a pirate costume, and the ornate letters of the caption read, GILBERT AND SULLIVAN'S THE PIRATES OF PENZANCE.

Mr. Galway turned the page. "Got several of these,

because I was so proud of the job I did with that theater. Here's me and Harry Houdini. And here's . . . well, I'll be darned."

He had stopped at a picture that showed a younger Mr. Galway, with a full head of dark hair and a big moustache, standing in front of the stairs outside the Seed & Feed. The building looked about the same, except for a large sign over the stair doorway that proclaimed, THE NEW ZEBEDEE OPERA HOUSE. Mr. Galway stared at the picture and scratched his head. "Well, I'll be. Guess my memory is playing tricks. I could have sworn that Immanuel Vanderhelm was in this picture with me, but I'm all by myself." He flipped back to *The Pirates of Penzance* photo. "Anyway, here is my first wife, Coral," he said.

Lewis suddenly leaned forward. He put his finger on a man in the front row. "Who is this?" he asked.

"That tall drink of water?" said Mr. Galway with a grin. "That's old Mordecai Finster, the theater manager. He's the one who skipped town later on, just before Vanderhelm's show flopped."

Lewis felt sick. He did not think that Mordecai Finster had skipped town. Something worse had happened to him. The man in the photo was tall and thin, with deep-set eyes and bushy muttonchop whiskers. Lewis had seen that figure before.

It was the ghost in the orchestra pit.

# CHAPTER FOUR

On Tuesday afternoon Jonathan Barnavelt stood at the window of his room in Lucius Mickleberry's house in St. Petersburg, Florida. He looked out on a gorgeous day. The Gulf of Mexico was calm and blue, and the white-sand beach he could glimpse between the trees was blinding in the warm sunshine. He had the telephone to his ear, and he was speaking to the long-distance operator. "New Zebedee," he repeated. "The number is 865."

He waited while the connection went through, and then he heard the phone ringing. After a moment there was a click and Mrs. Holtz said, "Hello, Barnavelt residence."

"Hi, Hannah," said Jonathan. "How is everything?"

"Oh, hello. Fine, thank you, Jonathan. Did you attend your friend's funeral?"

"It was a memorial service," Jonathan said. "Yes, it was very nice. I think Lucius would have liked it."

"We never know when it will be our time," said Mrs. Holtz dolefully.

Jonathan grinned. For a lively little woman, Mrs. Holtz took an uncommon interest in funerals. "Say, is Lewis there?" he asked. "I thought I'd speak to him if he's home from school."

"Yes, just a minute."

Jonathan hummed to himself. He saw Mrs. Zimmermann out on the lawn. She had changed from the black dress she had worn to the memorial service to a purple floral print, and she wore a white straw hat with a bright purple band. A balmy Gulf breeze blew, billowing her dress around her. She looked up, and Jonathan waved at her.

"Hello?" It was Lewis, sounding winded.

"Hi," Jonathan said. "Everything all right on the home front?"

There was a long pause, but then Lewis said, "Everything is fine. How is the weather?"

"Beautiful," Jonathan said. "It's about seventy-five degrees and sunny. How about there?"

"Cloudy, windy, and cold," Lewis said. "Do you know when you'll be back?"

"Not yet. We are meeting with the lawyers for the reading of the will tomorrow, and then Florence and I will have to sort out and pack books and other material.

That will take some time. And we need to have the wand-breaking."

"The what?" asked Lewis.

"It's a ceremony," his uncle explained. "You see, when a wizard dies through the action of magic, his wand breaks automatically. When a wizard dies a natural death, though, as Lucius did, then his magical friends have a little farewell creremony. They remember him and wish him well and then snap his wand in two. If my plane crashed while I was coming back to New Zebedee—"

"Gosh, Uncle Jonathan, don't even say that!" Lewis sounded strained and fearful.

Jonathan sighed. "Lewis, nothing like that is going to happen. I'm just using it as an example. Then my friends would break my walking cane. Florence's would break her enchanted umbrella. It's just a ceremony, that's all."

"Well . . . be careful anyway."

Jonathan laughed. "I will. Say, is everything all right at school? Did you and Rose Rita find a history project?"

"Uh, yes."

"Good, good. Well, I'll go now, Lewis. Tell you what: I'll shop around down here and see if I can find you a present. The pirate Gasparilla used to operate in these waters. Maybe I can find you a real doubloon or maybe a genuine pirate's sword."

"That would be swell."

"Take care then."

"You too."

Jonathan hung up and went downstairs to talk to Mrs.

Zimmermann. She had walked far out on the lawn, toward a gate that led out to the beach. As he stepped off the porch to follow her, Jonathan paused for a second. Something was troubling him. Lewis could be moody at times, but he had sounded subdued and depressed. Jonathan had the feeling that Lewis had never quite gotten over his parents' sudden death in a car accident several years earlier. However, Mrs. Holtz had sounded well enough, and she would have mentioned any real problems. Jonathan put his momentary worry out of his mind and trotted after Mrs. Zimmermann, yelling, "Hey, Haggy, wait up!"

Back in New Zebedee, Lewis hung up the phone and bit his lip. He had almost told his uncle about exploring the old theater, about seeing the ghost, and about the concealed sheet music. Two concerns stopped him. First, Lewis had to admit that he might have been mistaken. His nerves sometimes got the better of him, and it could be that the ghost of Mr. Finster was just a figment of his overactive imagination. Still, Lewis could not explain the resemblance between the man in Mr. Galway's picture album and what he thought he had seen in the orchestra pit. More important, though, was the fact that Lewis did not want to spoil Jonathan's stay in Florida. He knew his uncle had a lot on his mind, and he did not want to add to his problems.

When Mrs. Holtz had called him to the phone, Lewis had been sitting at the dining-room table, snacking on Reese's Peanut Butter Cups and a glass of milk. He went back there now and finished the candy, thinking over what had happened at school. Miss Fogarty had liked Rose Rita's description of the project she and Lewis had chosen, so it looked as if he would be stuck with researching the old theater. And Miss White, the music teacher, had been very interested in the old music score. She had explained that Immanuel Vanderhelm was once a world-famous tenor, and she was excited to think that this might be a long-lost work by the eminent musician. In fact, she had even telephoned the editor of the New Zebedee *Chronicle* with the news. Lewis thought things were getting out of hand.

The doorbell rang, and Lewis went to answer it. It was Rose Rita, her face red from the cold. "Look at this," she said, holding up a folded newspaper.

Lewis took it from her as she came in and closed the door. Right on the front page was a boxed story with a headline that read, NEW ZEBEDEE YOUTHS DISCOVER LOST OPERA. It told all about Lewis and Rose Rita and their finding the score to *The Day of Doom* in the old theater. It wound up by stating, "The opera is a parable of the modern world, showing how the new century meant the doom of all the old ways. According to Miss Ophelia White, the score seems to be complete and could even be performed now."

"We're famous," said Rose Rita with a grin. "Boy, I'll bet Miss Fogarty will *have* to give us both an *A* on this report!"

"Maybe," Lewis said uncertainly. "I don't like it, though."

They were still standing in the hall, next to the blue willowware vase that was crammed full of umbrellas and walking sticks. Rose Rita put her hands on her hips. "Humph! You just don't like it because you got scared."

"No," insisted Lewis. "It isn't that . . . it's just . . . oh, I don't know. It doesn't *feel* right to me, somehow. It's as if that stupid music had been in hiding there all this time, waiting for me to come along and find it. I know that sounds dumb, but it bothers me."

"Hey, relax," said Rose Rita. She was about half a head taller than Lewis, though he was going through what Jonathan called a growth spurt, and she looked down at him now. "You know, the music is even kind of pretty. Miss White played a few lines of the overture for me, and it doesn't sound spooky or weird—"

Rose Rita broke off, a funny look on her face. Lewis started to ask, "What is it?" Before he could get the words out, his voice died in his throat. He heard something. It was coming from outside, and it was high-pitched and wavery. It sounded like music being played on a fife, although he could not make out the tune. He shivered. "You hear that?" he whispered.

Rose Rita nodded, her eyes wide behind her glasses. "It's coming from the yard," she said. "You don't suppose it could be the, I mean, the ghost you . . ."

Suddenly Lewis relaxed and laughed. He had recognized the tune. It was "Goodnight, Ladies," and every sixth or seventh note was horribly flat. He went to the door, paused with his hand on the knob, and said, "Rose

Rita, meet the Phantom of the New Zebedee Opera!"
Then he threw the door wide.

A black-and-white striped cat came strolling in from the cold. He looked up at Rose Rita, meowed, and sat down to wash himself. "I don't get it," said Rose Rita.

"Didn't I tell you about Jailbird?" asked Lewis. "Gee, I thought I had. Last spring Uncle Jonathan and I were out in the yard when this cat showed up. We later found out he belongs to Miss Geer, the librarian, but we didn't know it then. Uncle Jonathan cast a magic spell on him, just for fun, and the cat started to whistle."

Rose Rita gave him a hard stare. "You're kidding."

"No," said Lewis. "It's the truth."

As if to demonstrate, Jailbird suddenly puckered his little cat lips and began to whistle "I'll Take You Home Again, Kathleen."

Rose Rita winced. "He's awful," she said.

Lewis shrugged. "Well, cats don't have much of a sense of pitch, Uncle Jonathan says. Anyhow, Jailbird seemed to like his new talent so much that Uncle Jonathan said he wouldn't take the spell off unless he started to do birdcalls. Last summer, while you were gone to Pennsylvania and Uncle Jonathan and I were off in Europe, Miss Geer took him to the radio studio talent contest, but they disqualified him because they said nobody at home would believe it was really a cat whistling, and anyway he wasn't very good."

The cat began a terrible off-key rendition of "On Top of Old Smoky."

"Can't you make him stop?" asked Rose Rita with a grimace.

"Sure. He just wants a snack." Lewis led them into the kitchen, where he opened a can of sardines. Jailbird gobbled them down and went to the heating vent, where he curled up contentedly. Lewis washed the special saucer that Jonathan used for giving handouts to neighborhood pets, and the cat purred as if pleased that Lewis was doing all the work. Then he softly whistled a few bars of Brahms's "Lullabye" before going to sleep. "I guess it will wear off sooner or later," Lewis said. "Most of Uncle Jonathan's spells do. You know the Fuse-Box Dwarf is gone. It gradually faded away, and then one day it just wasn't there anymore."

Rose Rita rolled her eyes. The Fuse-Box Dwarf had been another of Jonathan's spells. It was an illusion of a little man who lived behind the paint cans in the cellar, and when anyone went down there, he would rush out yelling, "Dreeb! Dreeb! I am the Fuse-Box Dwarf!" and then go hide again. "Your uncle doesn't do very useful magic," said Rose Rita.

"At least it's all harmless," returned Lewis. He really didn't feel like an argument. His head ached a little, and he was still nervous about the theater and the music he had found there. But Rose Rita seemed to understand. The two did their homework together, and when Rose Rita went home, Jailbird left as well. Lewis and Mrs. Holtz had dinner together, and then Lewis listened to some radio shows. He went to bed about nine o'clock, wishing that his uncle would return.

That night he tossed restlessly, unable to get to sleep for a long time. When at last he did fall asleep, he had a strange dream. He and Rose Rita were walking up the stairs to the theater again, but this time the lights were all on and a crowd was jostling them. The men wore black tailcoats and white ties, and they all carried top hats. The women wore long white gowns, beautiful necklaces of diamonds and pearls, and fur stoles around their shoulders.

Somehow Lewis and Rose Rita found themselves in the auditorium, which looked rich and elegant in the warm glow of a sparkling glass chandelier. A red velvet curtain with gold fringe hid the stage, and mournful music rose from the orchestra pit. This music summoned Lewis, and he plodded forward like a sleepwalker until he could look down into the pit.

The light gleamed off brass horns, dark woodwinds, and satiny violins that were lying on chairs or leaning against them. The grand piano was gone, and in its place stood an imposing organ. A man sat in front of it, his long, spidery fingers flying over the keys as he played the mysterious music. Slowly his head turned. For a moment Lewis was afraid he would see the dead face of the ghost again, but this was a different person, although he was as cadaverous as the ghost had been. He grinned at them. "Check your heads at the hatcheck counter!" he called pleasantly. "We'll have no whistling cats here. This is Art!"

As he laughed at his own words, a cloud of black flying things whirled out of his opened mouth. At first Lewis thought they were flies, but they grew larger and larger until they were bats, and they came flapping and squeaking right at him!

He and Rose Rita turned and ran up the aisle, but it was full of people now, who were shambling forward blindly. Lewis blinked hard. They were all headless! The men's collars ended with nothing above them. The bejeweled necks of the women were cut off above the pearls and diamonds. Rose Rita screamed.

The music grew louder and louder behind them. "If you want a tune, you have to pay the piper!" screeched the voice of the organist, and the black cloud of squeaking bats descended on Lewis, driving him to the floor. He lost sight of Rose Rita as he crawled frantically between the legs of the lurching, headless crowd. He had almost made it to the doorway leading to the vestibule when two balls came bouncing toward him.

Only they weren't balls. They were the heads of Jonathan Barnavelt and Mrs. Zimmermann, and their faces grimaced in terror. They rolled toward Lewis, their teeth snapping and clicking as if they were going to bite him.

Lewis scrambled back. Fingers clutched at his hair, and he heard the organist shriek, "Check this for you, sir?" Powerful hands tugged at his head. For a moment his neck seemed to stretch like taffy, and then he heard a sharp pop as everything went black.

# CHAPTER FIVE

All the rest of that week Lewis had similar horrifying dreams. Rose Rita had a few herself, but she blamed Lewis for them. "If you wouldn't go on and on about all this creepy stuff, I wouldn't think about it all the time," she complained. That made Lewis angry, and the two didn't speak to each other much until after school on Friday. That was when Miss White planned to play a few selections from the opera score for five or six specially invited guests, as well as for the two friends. When school ended, Lewis hung around, miserable, drained, and tired from the nightmares that kept him awake at night. Jonathan had called again on Thursday afternoon to say that he and Mrs. Zimmermann would need about ten more days to catalog everything and arrange to have it shipped to New Zebedee. Again Lewis kept himself from mentioning his fears. After all, nothing awful had happened, except for his bad dreams.

And Rose Rita's. She looked as exhausted as Lewis felt. "Have another one?" he asked cautiously. They liked each other too much to keep the silent treatment up for very long. She sighed.

The two of them were sitting at the back of the music room, a light and airy place with rows of chairs instead of desks. Music stands stood here and there, and a permanent border around the top of the blackboard showed the music staves and the various markings that went on them. The bass and treble clefs were drawn in yellow and white chalk, along with the musical notations from a full note to an eighth. An upright piano sat in front of the blackboard. The whole room smelled of chalk dust and disinfectant. Rose Rita finally admitted, "I had a bad one last night. I dreamed I was being chased by all these whistling cats that wanted me to teach them the score of *The Day of Doom*. They chased me right into a long dark tunnel. And then they somehow sealed off both the exits—ugh!"

Lewis nodded sympathetically. Rose Rita was a lot braver then he was, but a few things terrified her. One was any closed-in space. Rose Rita couldn't stand being in dark closets or tunnels, and she looked distressed just telling the dream to Lewis. He sighed and said, "Mine wasn't that bad, I guess. I thought I was in the theater again, watching Harry Houdini and Enrico Caruso do magic tricks while they sang 'Take Me Out to the Ball Game.' Then I noticed that everyone around me was a ghost. Mr. Finster, the theater manager, was there, and lots and lots of others too. None of them were looking at the stage. They were all staring at me, and their eyes were round and empty, like Little Orphan Annie's in the funny papers. Then they all started to whisper to me."

"What were they saying?" asked Rose Rita. She had dark circles under her eyes, and she could not keep from yawning.

"It was hard to tell at first," said Lewis. "But it kept getting louder until it sounded like the wind on a stormy day. They were all saying, 'Stop the voices! Stop the voices!' over and over again. I tried to get up to leave, but I couldn't move. When I looked down at my body, I had turned into a ghost myself, and I was doomed to sit there in the theater forever."

They heard voices in the hall, and a moment later Miss White came in with a group of people. Lewis gulped in surprise. He recognized the portly, white-haired Mr. Davis, the mayor of New Zebedee, and Mr. and Mrs. Paulson, who published the New Zebedee *Chronicle*. They were a tubby middle-aged couple who looked a lot alike, both with graying black hair and double chins. Fussy Principal Potter was talking to them. There were also two women and two men whom Lewis did not recognize, but Miss White was chatting away to them all. "And," she said as they stood at the front of the room, "here are our heroes, the ones who made this marvelous discovery. Stand up, Rose Rita and Lewis."

Both of them rose, although Lewis, at least, felt foolish doing so. The grown-ups smiled and nodded at them and murmured polite greetings. Then Miss White asked everyone to find a seat. "Feels just like we're in school again, eh, Letty?" Mr. Paulson asked his wife. She sniffed and did not bother to reply.

Miss White stood beside the piano. She was tall and thin and wore a tailored gray tweed skirt with a white blouse and a fussy little black bow at the neck. Her hair was a curly reddish-brown, and the teardrop-shaped lenses of her eyeglasses made her look like a cat. "I've asked you all here," she said, "to listen to a few selections from this masterpiece. I believe this magnum opus should be given to the world, and after you have heard a bit of it, I feel sure you will agree with me."

She sat at the keyboard, bowed her head for a moment, and then looked up. "This is an aria from Act One of *The Day of Doom*," she said.

Mrs. Paulson sniffed again. "Not a very promising title, Ophelia," she observed.

"Oh, but it's very symbolic," replied Miss White in an eager voice. "It is all about the passing away of the old times of strife and war and hatred and the dawning of a new era of peace and cooperation."

"Well, well, let's hear it, Miss White," said the mayor. "I am a very busy man, you know, and I'm sure everyone else has other things to do too."

"This is the aria. It is called simply 'The Summoning,'" said Miss White, and she began to play.

The music started out very delicately, a plaintive, rather monotonous melody. Lewis gave Rose Rita a look that said, What is the big deal? Rose Rita just shrugged in response, raising her eyebrows to show that she didn't get it either. Gradually the music became stronger and more insistent. Lewis listened to it, but he did not particularly care for it. He was not much of a fan of any kind of music, not even bebop. Occasionally his uncle would tune their big Atwater-Kent radio to musical programs such as "The WLS Barn Dance" or "The Grand Ole Opry," which played country tunes, cowboy music, and square-dance melodies. They were nothing like the aria that Miss White now performed. Lewis wrinkled up his nose. He was bored, and itching to go home.

He noticed, though, that the adults appeared to like the music a lot. They nodded and even swayed a little in time to the hypnotic beat, and they leaned forward in their chairs as Miss White brought the tune to a crescendo. When she stopped playing, they all applauded heartily. "By golly, Miss White," said Mayor Davis, "I'll confess that I didn't half believe you when you told us how good this thing was, but you were right. This Immanuel Vanderhelm must have been a genius."

"Indeed," said Mrs. Paulson, beaming. "I have seldom heard a more satisfying, yet simple composition. It has all the grace and charm of Mozart, with the esprit of Vivaldi and the élan of Beethoven."

"You played good too," observed her husband.

"Why, thank you."

They all started discussing the best way to make the music public. Mr. Paulson thought that Miss White should just have a recital, but Mr. Davis shook his head at that. "This can be big," he said, "really big. We might get people in to hear this thing from Osee Five Hills, Kalamazoo, and Ann Arbor if we play our cards right. Why, we could make New Zebedee a tourist attraction."

"How?" someone else asked, sounding puzzled.

"Why, we could put on the show right here in town," said the mayor. "The Eleemosynary and Cultural League had a lease on the opera house. The League stopped meeting years ago, but there must be three or four of the members still in town. We just get them together, let them vote to reopen the theater, and there you are."

"Take a lot of work to get that place back into operating order," one of the other men said. "And where's the money comin' from, Hugo? That's what I'd like to know."

They all started to wrangle then, and Rose Rita tugged Lewis's arm. The two of them slipped out of the room. "Whew!" said Lewis. "I'll bet they stay there all night arguing about that stupid opera."

"I don't know," replied Rose Rita thoughtfully. "The music *was* kind of pretty."

"Ugh," said Lewis. "Deedle, deedle, doopty-doo! I'd rather hear Jailbird whistling."

They went downstairs and opened the side door. The junior high was a black stone building next to the high school, and this door opened out into a narrow alley. The day was cool, but the weather had moderated a little, and the ice and snow that had accumulated in February and early March were melting. The air smelled sharp and a little muddy—the smell of spring coming,

Jonathan always said of it. Lewis and Rose Rita walked around to the back of the school to get their bikes.

"Who's that?" Rose Rita asked as they rode out of the alley. A man in a long black overcoat stood in front of the school. He wore a black homburg and black leather gloves, and his overcoat had a collar and lapels of some spotted white fur. The man had a neatly trimmed black beard, and he carried a newspaper. Lewis did not recognize him, but he thought the man looked foreign.

"Children!" the stranger said as he caught sight of them. His voice was hearty and strong. "Maybe you can give me a little help. Is this the school where the students found an old opera score last week?"

"Sure is," Rose Rita said. "In fact, we're the ones who found it. I'm Rose Rita Pottinger, and this is Lewis Barnavelt."

"Really?" the man asked with a delighted smile. "How fortunate I met you, then. I understand you were exploring some theater when you made the discovery."

"That's right," said Rose Rita. "The New Zebedee Opera House. Only it's been closed for years and years, because Harry Houdini came through once and made a daring escape while handcuffed underwater, and then two boys from town tried it and drowned. Everyone loved those boys, and the town was so sad that they just boarded the old place up."

Lewis stared at Rose Rita in shock. He liked her a lot, but she always preferred stories that were dramatic and interesting, and she didn't mind embroidering them a little to make them sound better. He almost told Rose

Rita to knock it off, but he was timid in front of the tall, bearded stranger.

But the man appeared to take Rose Rita's story seriously. "My, my, that is dreadful. However, I am very happy that you two bright children discovered that old score. You see, my name is Henry Vanderhelm, and my grandfather wrote the piece."

"Immanuel Vanderhelm," Lewis said. "That was the name on the cover sheet."

"Indeed, as you say, Immanuel Vanderhelm, a multi-talented gentleman of considerable renown," replied the man. "He was, as I am, a singer. Alas, I inherited only a fraction of his great abilities, and my success has been moderate. Still, my father told me many stories of my illustrious ancestor's wonderful career, and I would dearly love to hear his work."

"Well, gee," Rose Rita said, "you're in luck. Miss White is inside, and she has the whole score on her piano."

"Ah. Perhaps you two would be good enough to take me there?" When the two hesitated, Vanderhelm added coaxingly, "You see, a gentleman cannot simply strike up a conversation with a lady without a proper introduction. I would be grateful if you would introduce us."

Lewis swallowed. For some reason he did not much care for the idea of going back into the school. But he could not put his finger on the problem, and so he just nodded.

"Splendid," said Vanderhelm. "Lead on! And I hope it doesn't call for a bicycle, because I left mine at the

National House Hotel." He smiled to show he was joking.

They went back in the side door and upstairs. As they walked down the hall toward the room, Lewis could hear the adults squabbling. The door was open. Mr. Vanderhelm did not wait for his introduction, but stepped swiftly ahead of Lewis and Rose Rita and entered the room.

Mr. Paulson was saying, "Hang it, it may be a good idea, but where are we s'posed to get the talent to perform an opera around here?"

He broke off and fell silent as Mr. Vanderhelm came into the room, his overcoat swirling like a cape. "Perform the opera?" he boomed in his rich voice. "You wish to perform my grandfather's opera?"

Miss White rose from her seat at the piano, pressing her hand against her chest and looking as if she were about to faint. Mr. Davis asked, "Your grandfather's opera? You mean you're—"

Vanderhelm bowed with a grand sweep. "I am Henry Vanderhelm, baritone, sir. And I have the honor to be the grandson of the world-famous tenor, musician, and composer Immanuel Vanderhelm. I believe you were discussing my grandfather's work as I came in?"

"Uh-oh," said Mr. Paulson. "There goes our bright idea. I suppose you own the rights to the opera now?"

Vanderhelm waved a black-gloved hand. "The world owns the right to hear it, sir. Oh, please have no worry on my account. Your enthusiasm for my grandfather's work fills me with an indescribable pleasure. You wish to perform *The Day of Doom* in New Zebedee? Wonderful! In fact, I—if you will have one so humble—I myself am prepared to stage, direct, and appear in the work, all at my own expense."

Mr. Paulson immediately began to applaud, and everyone joined in. Even Rose Rita clapped. Only Lewis did not join in. He did not clap because something had startled and perplexed him. Lewis was quite sure that Mr. Vanderhelm had been holding a copy of the New Zebedee *Chronicle* when he and Rose Rita first saw the man. The black overcoat had no pockets. Vanderhelm had not tossed the newspaper into a wastebasket or laid it down anywhere in the room, and yet both his hands were empty.

Where had the paper gone? It had simply vanished.

Like a ghost, Lewis thought, and goosebumps rose on his arms.

# CHAPTER SIX

"Mr. Vanderhelm then sang a powerful tune called 'The Sealing' from the opera, to general approbation," read Rose Rita aloud. It was Sunday afternoon, and she and Lewis were sitting at the dining-room table in the Barnavelt house. Mr. Paulson had run a prominent story in the Sunday paper about Henry Vanderhelm and the opera, complete with a large photo of the man himself, looking confident and happy as Miss White and Letty Paulson gazed adoringly at him from either side.

"You don't have to read that," growled Lewis, who was trying to concentrate on "Dick Tracy" and "Li'l Abner" in the comics. "I was there, remember?"

Rose Rita rattled the paper and looked over the top of the page at Lewis. Her expression was grim. "So was I—*remember*? But this is interesting. According to this story, there were a few other developments yesterday, when the city fathers and the school board met with Mr. Vanderhelm. But I guess you're not interested in news, Mr. Know-It-All."

"Rose Rita, I don't *like* all this," muttered Lewis. "I wish we'd never gone into the opera house in the first place. Everything that's happened since then feels sort of funny. I mean funny weird, not funny ha-ha. I wish Uncle Jonathan was back. He'd know what to do." He sighed. "I guess we'd better get our math assignment done."

"I'm not doing it," returned Rose Rita smugly.

"Oh, come on," said Lewis. "Look, I know you're mad at me, but let bygones be bygones, okay? Anyway, we have to start on the math now, because Mrs. Holtz insists on going to evening Mass, and I'll have to tag along for that."

"Why do math?" Rose Rita asked sweetly. "There's no point in it."

Lewis glowered at her. "Okay, smarty," he said. "I'll do my math homework, and if you have trouble with it, don't come crying to me."

"There's no point in your doing math either," Rose Rita informed him with an annoying smile.

"What are you talking about? Come on, I'm in no mood for all this," complained Lewis.

"Well, you didn't want to hear the rest of the story," said Rose Rita. "If you'd let me read it, you would know that the school board has cancelled classes for next week so that Mr. Vanderhelm can use the school for auditions."

"What?" Lewis grabbed the paper from Rose Rita and read the story. It was true. Mr. Vanderhelm had announced his intention to begin tryouts on Monday, and the school board had suspended classes not only in the junior high but in the high school as well. Parents had volunteered to clean and spruce up the old theater, the article said. Lewis dropped the paper and stared at Rose Rita. Normally he would welcome such news; like any kid, he was always happy when a blizzard forced school to close for a day or two. This, however, struck him as all wrong.

Rose Rita looked troubled too, now that her little bout of teasing him was over. "People are acting crazy," she said. "School boards just don't do stuff like this. I'm worried."

Lewis's mouth was dry. "I had another bad dream last night," he mumbled.

"Me too."

They looked at each other for a long time. Timidly, Lewis said, "Friends again?"

"Sure," said Rose Rita, smiling. Then she shuddered a little. "I wish Mrs. Zimmermann was back. She'd know what to do about all this."

Lewis made up his mind. "Let's call Uncle Jonathan," he said. "He left me the number of Mr. Mickleberry's house, where he and Mrs. Zimmermann are staying. I think they ought to know what's been happening."

Lewis got the number from his room, and they went into the study. Lewis slipped into his uncle's chair and lifted the receiver. The operator said, "Number, please?" in a pleasant, cheerful voice.

"Uh, this is a long-distance call," Lewis said. He then gave the operator the information. The line clicked and crackled with a little static for a few moments. Then the operator came back on to say, "I am sorry. I cannot get a clear line to Florida at the moment. Will you try your call again later?"

"Yes, thank you," said Lewis. He hung up glumly. "Can't get through," he explained to Rose Rita.

"That's funny," Rose Rita said, frowning. "I mean, your Uncle Jonathan got through to you a couple of times. I wonder what's wrong?"

"Who knows?" Lewis said. He drummed his fingers on the desk. "Well, we can wait an hour or so and then try again. I guess we don't have to worry about home-work. Want to play some chess?"

They got the chessboard out and set it up on the dining-room table. The board was one of Jonathan's lit-tle indulgences. It was made of leather, and the squares were ivory and brown instead of red and black. The chessmen matched the board, with one set carved from ordinary white marble and one from a deep chocolate-colored marble that could be found in only one obscure quarry in Lombardy, a region in northern Italy. Jonathan had cast a spell on the chessmen, so that they were able to comment on the action. When a knight was moved to a position where it threatened another piece, it would say, "Have at thee for a foul faytour, varlet!" And whenever a pawn was captured, it would shriek, "Aggh! Ya got me, pal!" in a tiny, high-pitched voice. Rose Rita finally won when she managed to move her queen to a checkmate position. "That's all for you, Big Boy," said the queen in Mae West's voice. Lewis's defeated brown king muttered, "Mother of Mercy, is this the end of Little Caesar?" and tipped itself over.

They tried to telephone Jonathan and Mrs. Zimmermann once more, but again the operator could not get a long-distance line. By that time Mrs. Holtz was preparing dinner, so Rose Rita left. Lewis wandered around the house for awhile, feeling adrift and vaguely apprehensive. He went to the back stairs in the south wing and stared at the oval stained-glass window, the one that changed every time he looked at it. Today it showed a milk-white angel playing a golden harp as she flew through a sky the exact color of a Vicks VapoRub jar. That reminded Lewis of the magic hat stand in the hallway, and he went to take a look at it.

The hat stand had a small round mirror in it, and sometimes this mirror showed strange, faraway scenes. In the glass Lewis had seen Mayan pyramids, a part of the Battle of New Orleans, and even the horrid landscape of the dread planet Yuggoth as it rolled through the midnight gulfs between the stars. He stared at the mirror for awhile. At first he could see only his face, a little pudgy and exhausted looking. Then suddenly he was looking at a blue sea rippling with foamy waves. A white-sand beach lay in the warm sunshine, and fronds of date palms swayed gently back and forth in a gentle breeze. A big beach umbrella stood in the sand, and under it were two beach towels, one purple and one white. Lewis squinted. Two tiny figures were on the towels. One had white hair and wore an old-fashioned purple bathing suit. She was reading a book that was propped on her knees. The other was lying on his stomach, apparently asleep. He wore an orange tank top and navy-blue trunks. Lewis grinned. It was Mrs. Zimmermann and Uncle Jonathan.

Just then Mrs. Holtz called him to dinner, and Lewis looked away to answer. When he returned his gaze to the mirror, he could see only himself. He felt a little better, though, and he went to the dining room in a more cheerful frame of mind.

The next morning Lewis woke up and blinked at the Westclox alarm clock on his bedside table. Seven-thirty! He jumped out of bed in a panic and had started to scramble into his clothes when he suddenly remembered that he had turned off the alarm the night before. There was no school today. With a sigh of relief, Lewis showered and dressed more slowly. When he came downstairs, Mrs. Holtz had breakfast ready: home fries, scrambled eggs, and raisin-bran muffins. The housekeeper was almost as good a cook as Mrs. Zimmermann, and the food smelled delicious.

Mrs. Holtz was standing at the counter, fiddling with the knobs on her Motorola radio. She liked to listen to the news and weather on the Chicago station WLS at breakfast time, but now she was frowning and muttering to herself. "Hi, Mrs. Holtz," said Lewis as he slipped into his chair and began to help himself to the eggs and potatoes. "What's wrong?"

"Oh, this blamed thing is on the fritz," said Mrs. Holtz as she gave the radio a sharp slap. "I couldn't pick up Chicago, so I was trying to get the Grand Rapids station, but all the set's picking up today is WNZB." WNZB was the New Zebedee radio station. Until about nine o'clock all you could get on it were farm reports and the Swap Club, a call-in show for people with items for sale such as old toasters, newborn piglets, or pick-up trucks that needed new engines and a little bodywork. It was pretty boring stuff. Mrs. Holtz finally gave up and sat at the table. She had already eaten, but she had another cup of coffee and looked uncharacteristically grumpy at missing her favorite morning programs.

After breakfast Lewis went into the study and tried his uncle's radio. It was a large floor model, with a round dial the size of a dinner plate on which there were nine separate radio bands. You could listen to regular broadcasts, or tune to shortwave bands and hear strange, distant stations with announcers who spoke in many different langauges. You could hear the weather, police calls, and airplane bands, where pilots talked to their control towers. There were even amateur bands, for ham-radio operators to chat with their pals in far-flung corners of the globe.

This morning, all Lewis could pick up on the radio was boring old WNZB. He frowned. Mrs. Holtz had thought something was wrong with her radio, but apparently that was not where the trouble lay. He sat at the desk and tried again to telephone his uncle, but as soon as he asked the operator for the number, she said, "I'm sorry, but we have no long-distance lines at the moment. Will you try your call again later?"

Lewis began to get a creepy feeling. He asked Mrs. Holtz for permission to go visit Rose Rita, and she told him to go ahead and to be polite. Lewis got into his coat and rode his bike over to Mansion Street, where Rose Rita lived. Mrs. Pottinger called Rose Rita, and the two went into the living room. The Pottingers had a TV set, but when Lewis and Rose Rita tried it, they got only snow. "Something weird is going on," Lewis said anxiously.

Rose Rita bit her lip. "Dad was furious this morning because the Detroit paper didn't come. What do you suppose all this means?"

"How should I know?" asked Lewis.

"You're the one who likes to pretend to be Sherlock Holmes," Rose Rita shot back. Then she looked embarrassed. "I'm sorry. I don't want to fight. It's just that all this is making me nervous."

Lewis thought for a moment. "Tell you what," he said. "We can't get an outside phone line from New Zebedee, but I'll bet we could if we rode our bikes out to Eldridge Corners. There's a pay phone at the gas station, and it's on the Homer exchange, not the New Zebedee one."

"That's a pretty long way to ride," said Rose Rita doubtfully. It was about five miles out to Eldridge Corners, on the winding Homer Road.

"What else do we have to do?" responded Lewis. "There's no school today."

"Okay," said Rose Rita. "Let me tell my mom that we're going out."

Rose Rita made them a picnic lunch of ham sandwiches, an apple apiece, and some Oreo cookies, and she got a couple of bottles of pop from the refrigerator. She stowed the provisions in the saddlebags of her bike, and they were off.

It was almost spring, and the weather had become much warmer over the past week. Some ice and snow lingered where there was deep shade, but the air, though still nippy, wasn't nearly as frigid as it had been. The sky was clear and blue with bright sunshine. Rose Rita and Lewis rode their bikes downtown, and on Main Street they passed to look at the Feed & Seed. A couple of tall ladders leaned against the brick wall, and some high-school boys were attaching a sign to some iron hooks set into the bricks. The New Zebedee Opera House read the freshly painted green-and-yellow sign. A banner had been attached to the bottom of it. In neat red capital letters it proclaimed Grand Reopening Soon!

Rose Rita and Lewis looked at one another. Then they rode toward the railway tracks, where the Homer Road joined Main Street. They had clattered across the tracks and past the athletic field, when suddenly they ran into a fog bank. The whole world became gray as they plunged into it, and Lewis could barely see Rose Rita ahead to the left of him. He couldn't see anything else at all, not even the ground. "This is a strange kind of fog," Rose Rita said as she slowed her bike. "It's so clear everywhere else—it's thinning out again, though."

For a few seconds they had been riding through a blinding, heavy mist as thick as soup. Then it brightened and became less dense. All of a sudden, their bikes jolted over railroad tracks.

Lewis braked, feeling panic rising in his chest. They were heading back into town. Somehow they had turned completely around, although he knew he had not swerved. "How'd we do this?" asked Rose Rita.

Lewis did not reply. He turned his bike and started out of town again, and Rose Rita followed. She almost banged into him moments later. Their bikes rattled over the tracks, and they found themselves right back where they started, again heading into town.

"We're trapped," Lewis said, fighting the urge to scream. "We can't get out of town—and I'll bet nobody else can get into New Zebedee either. That's why your dad's paper didn't come this morning."

Rose Rita stared at him with wide, frightened eyes. "And we can't get any out-of-town radio or TV stations," she said. In a shaky voice she asked, "Lewis, do you suppose something has happened to the outside world? Is New Zebedee all there is *left*?"

Lewis had not considered that, but now he did. And he became so frightened, he thought he might lose his mind.

# CHAPTER SEVEN

The disturbing fog hung in a circle all around New Zebedee. As Lewis and Rose Rita tested the boundaries, they found they could not get beyond the city limits on the Homer Road or on routes 9 or 12. They got a little farther going cross-country through Wilder Creek Park. In fact, they left the park behind and started up Cemetery Hill, where they had to get off and walk their bikes. Oakridge Cemetery was south of town on a high, flat ridge that was cut across by two dirt roads. Rose Rita and Lewis paused to park their bikes under the gate of the cemetery. This was a heavy stone arch covered with elaborate carving. On the lintel over their heads were inscribed these words:

*The trumpet shall sound*
*and*
*the dead shall be raised*

Lewis felt his knees trembling. He had avoided the cemetery for years. Years ago, he and a boy named Tarby Corrigan had come here on Halloween at midnight. Lewis had been trying to show off, and he cast a necromancy spell—a spell meant to raise the dead—outside the Izard tomb. He still had nightmares about what had come out of that sinister mausoleum.

"Look at that," said Rose Rita in a voice filled with awe. They gazed down, over the bare black trees in the park and back at the town of New Zebedee. To their left and right, long arms of gray fog swept in on either side of the town, right along the city limits. They could not see beyond the town, but Lewis was willing to bet that the fog was there too. They could see nothing but fog everywhere, heavy, sluggish, and gray, like the underside of a stormcloud. That wasn't right. The sun had been shining, so the fog should have been brighter and lighter. Rose Rita sighed and climbed onto her bike. "Let's see if we can get out through the cemetery."

With his heart thumping hard, Lewis plodded after her down the dirt road. They passed a section of the cemetery where all the monuments were carved to look like logs, and they went through the area with statues of weeping women leaning on urns and cupids extinguishing torches. Ahead was the back fence of the cemetery, black wrought-iron curlicues with decorative spearheads every ten feet or so. And beyond that, the mysterious gray fog bank leaking wisps here and there. They retreated to the highest part of the cemetery, where Rose Rita climbed up the barred iron door of a mausoleum to stand on the roof. "It's no use," she called down. "We're surrounded."

She scrambled down and drew a diagram in the dirt with a stick to explain what she had seen. The fog was everywhere except in the cemetery and in New Zebedee itself. The clear places formed a lopsided figure 8, with the smaller loop of the 8 as the cemetery and the larger one the town. Lewis looked around fearfully. A gray stone statue down the hill, a woman in a cloak with a hood over her forehead, seemed to stare back at him. "What are we going to do?"

Rose Rita shook her head. "Don't ask me. We could climb the fence, but I have a feeling we wouldn't get anywhere through that fog. We'd probably just take a couple of steps away and then bang into the fence again."

Lewis groaned and turned away. He felt a chill creeping up his spine. The hooded statue was closer, wasn't it? He tried to remember where it had been before. Now it seemed to be striding forward, a grim look on its pitted stone face. Lewis stared at it, but it was not moving. He swallowed hard and turned back to Rose Rita. "It's the music, isn't it? When that Mr. Vanderhelm sang the song, he did something awful."

"It was called 'The Sealing,'" said Rose Rita in a thoughtful voice. "Maybe it did some kind of magic.

Like sealing the town off from the outside world, and vicy-versa, as your uncle would say."

Lewis blinked. "And the song that Miss White played first was called 'The Summoning.' That might have been what drew Henry Vanderhelm here in the first place."

"I wonder who he really is?" mused Rose Rita.

Lewis thought he knew. "It's him. It's old Immanuel Vanderhelm himself, come back to finish whatever it was he started back in 1919." He got the shakes and looked over his shoulder. His mouth dropped open.

Rose Rita considered this and shook her head. "I don't see how that's possible. Henry Vanderhelm can't be more than about thirty years old. I think he must be who he says he is—old Immanuel's grandson."

"R-Rose Rita," stammered Lewis, "L-look down the hill."

She frowned at him and then followed his trembling, pointing finger. "It's a momument. So what?"

"It's r-reaching out its arms toward us."

"It's beseeching the mercy of heaven or something," said Rose Rita firmly.

"I know it wasn't stretching its arms out before," insisted Lewis. "And it's closer now than it was."

"Maybe we'd better go," Rose Rita said. They started downhill. They passed the stone woman, and she was soon hidden from view behind mausoleums and other markers. Then Rose Rita squeaked in surprise and stopped suddenly.

Lewis groaned. There she was again, ahead of them now, leaning on a tombstone, her shoulders hunched.

The stone mouth had opened, and inside were two rows of sharp stone teeth. A forked tongue lolled out, and the hands clenching the tombstone ended in wicked, hooked claws. She was just beside the path.

"I think we'd better go the long way," Rose Rita said, her voice shaking. "Nobody would put up a memorial like that!"

They nearly ran for the main road, leaving the grotesque statue behind. The dirt road led down steeply to the stone arch where they had left their bikes. "Oh, no!" said Lewis. "Look up there!"

A huddled shape crouched on the arch, like a lion hunched waiting for the kill. They could see it only in silhouette, and it no longer looked very human, but Lewis knew in his heart that it was the moving statue, waiting for them.

"We can't stay here forever," whispered Rose Rita. "Look, we never see it move, right?"

"B-but it does move!"

"Let's try something. C'mon!" Rose Rita plunged into the stone forest of carved logs, with Lewis trotting desperately behind her. They came to a small clearing and stood back-to-back, peering around. "I see her," Rose Rita said grimly.

Lewis turned, feeling cold and weak. He saw the woman too, only she was no longer a woman but a—a *thing* perched on top of a tombstone carved like an upright log. Her toothy face had grown sharp-snouted and snakelike, her knotted arms impossibly long. The hood had become a cobra's hood, and she had no legs at all, just a long, coiling serpent's tail wrapped around and around the log she perched on. Her eyes looked alive now, glaring at them with hatred and hunger.

"I want you to back up to the main road," Rose Rita said, her voice shaky. "Don't take your eyes off me until you get there. And when I tell you, look straight at the gate. Tell me if she's gone."

"B-but there she is on the tombstone!" chattered Lewis.

"There may be *more than one*."

Lewis backed away, step after terrified step. He could not fight off the feeling that a hideous stone hand would close on his shoulder at any moment. But somehow he made it to the dirt road. "I'm here," he called, his voice shrill with dread.

"Look at the gate."

Lewis had to wrench his gaze downhill. His heart leaped. "She's not there!"

"Keep your eyes on the gate," Rose Rita yelled. "I'm coming toward you." Lewis heard her blundering, and in a moment she bumped into him. "I can still see her," said Rose Rita in a dismal voice. "But when we move downhill, I'll lose sight of her. You keep your eyes on the gate. I'll look back this way. If she can't let us see her move, we should be all right."

They inched downhill so slowly that Lewis thought they were hardly moving at all. He did not dare to blink. His feet scuffed the damp dirt. His eyes ached and watered. Closer and closer they came, until they were actually under the arch. "Get on your bike!" Rose Rita yelled. She leaped for hers too.

Lewis clambered on and found the pedals. They started away from the cemetery. From behind them grew a horrible, vicious snarl, like the frustrated cry of a hungry wolf whose prey had been just a little too fast. They flew down through the park and over the brook, and at last Rose Rita stopped and turned. "I think we're safe now. I don't think it can come out of the graveyard."

Lewis looked up the hill. He could not be sure, but he thought he saw a crouching shadow just inside the archway. "Why is it there?" he asked, his teeth clicking as if he were freezing.

"It's to keep us from getting in, I guess," said Rose Rita. "Or maybe," she swallowed hard, "maybe to keep the dead from getting *out*."

"What are we gonna do?" asked Lewis in agony.

"We need help," replied Rose Rita. "But who? I could tell my parents, but you know how *they* are."

Lewis nodded. George Pottinger was a nice man at heart, but he tended to be grumpy and skeptical. And Louise Pottinger was a kindly, absentminded woman who did not believe half the things Rose Rita told her anyway.

"How about your grandpa?" asked Lewis. "He might believe us."

Rose Rita shook her head. "He went to stay at my uncle's farm for the weekend. With this incredible fog, he couldn't have gotten back." She bit her lip. "I think old Vanderhelm has cast some kind of goofy spell over the grown-ups in town too. Half of them won't believe us, and the other half are probably under Vanderhelm's power."

Lewis had been thinking. "I know some grown-ups who'll listen. The Capharnaum County Magicians Society!"

"That's right!" said Rose Rita. "Why didn't I think of that? Do you know who they are?"

Lewis smiled. "My uncle is the treasurer, and he has the club ledger in his desk. It has a list of everyone who's paid dues and who hasn't, and all the names and addresses are right there in the front."

"Well, let's go!"

Their bikes fairly flew on the way back to 100 High Street. They pulled up in front of the old stone mansion and went pounding up the steps. The front door was locked, which meant Mrs. Holtz was probably out shopping. But Lewis had his own key. He and Rose Rita hurried to the study, and Lewis rummaged in the desk drawer until he pulled out a tall, skinny book, bound in green cloth, its corners reinforced with triangles of brown leather. He plopped it down on the desk and opened it, running his finger down a list of names. "Here!" he said. "Mrs. Zenobia Weatherly. She's the president of the society, and she lives over on West River Avenue."

"Call her," said Rose Rita. "Her number's 707."

Lewis tried, but the operator told him that the number

had been disconnected. He hung up with a sinking heart. He and Rose Rita wrote down Mrs. Weatherly's address, and the names and addresses of the society vice president and secretary. Then they went outside, climbed on their bikes, and rode over to West River Avenue.

They pulled up short at the place where Mrs. Weatherly was supposed to live. The house at 796 was a green clapboard cottage; the one at 800 was a neat white bungalow with a frisky fox terrier romping in front as two boys tossed a ball for him to fetch. Between them, where number 798 should have been, was a weed-choked vacant lot. From the knee-high yellow grass and dried stalks of lady's slipper, burdock, and other wild plants that grew, it would appear that no house had ever been built there.

Rose Rita and Lewis paused outside the picket fence where the kids were playing with the dog. They must have been twins, about eight years old, with identical blond crew cuts and tough faces. "Hey," called Rose Rita pleasantly, "can you tell us about Mrs. Weatherly?"

"Huh?" one of the boys asked. He came over and clung to the picket fence, looking over the points at Rose Rita and Lewis. "Mrs. Whosis?" he said.

"Mrs. Zenobia Weatherly," explained Rose Rita. "She's supposed to live next door at 798. Did she move or something?"

"You're crazy," the kid said. "Nobody lives next door. Nobody's ever lived next door. Just that old stinky lot there." He swung off the fence and grabbed the ball.

"C'mon, Tommy," he said. "We'll go an' play in the backyard, away from these crazy people." He ran around the side of the house.

The other boy, who did not appear as tough as his brother, lingered a moment. He looked at Lewis and Rose Rita with round, frightened blue eyes. "I *thought* somebody lived there," he whispered. "An ol' lady with gray hair. An' her house was a big brick place with a tower. But everybody says I just dreamed that." Then he ran after his brother.

Lewis and Rose Rita stared at each other. In a grave voice Rose Rita asked, "Who's next on the list?"

They checked the addresses where the vice president and the secretary were supposed to live, but the outcome was the same. Instead of houses, they found weedy vacant lots and the neighbors insisted that no houses had ever been there, although one old man looked troubled and uncertain even as he was shooing Lewis and Rose Rita away. The two rode their bikes over to St. George's Church, where Lewis attended Mass. They rested in the side yard of the church, sitting on a cool stone bench beneath a maple tree. "He's outfoxed us," admitted Rose Rita. "Old Vanderhelm didn't miss a trick. Somehow or other, he's done away with all the members of the Capharnaum County Magicians Society who might have helped us."

"Done away with them?" squeaked Lewis. "You don't mean—"

Rose Rita pushed her glasses into place on her nose and shrugged. "I don't think he's killed them, if that's what you're worried about. But he's sealed them off, somehow, just like he's sealed off the town. They're probably in their houses right now, wondering why it's foggy all around their yards and why they can't get to the store to buy a pound of butter."

"I hope so," said Lewis. He could hardly bear to think of what else might have happened to them. What if the spell had turned them into frogs or mice? What if they and their houses had been sent off to some bizarre planet, where the population was all made up of Mud Men and Bird Men and Tree Men, like in the *Flash Gordon* movie serials the Bijou sometimes showed on Saturday mornings? What if they found themselves in a world of horrible, living, changing stone statues? Or— Lewis tried to swallow the painful lump in his throat— or what if the spell had somehow just *erased* them, removed them from the world as if they had never existed?

"Well," said Rose Rita, breaking his gloomy train of thought, "I guess there's only one thing to do. I'll have to tell my mother about this. Would you come with me?"

"S-sure," Lewis said. "You know I will."

Rose Rita sighed. "Thanks. Mom is all right, but she thinks everything I tell her is a lie." After a moment she added in a small voice, "I guess I tell her too many stories."

Lewis realized that Rose Rita was on the verge of tears, and that shook him up more than anything else. Rose Rita was a very brave person. Unlike her, when Lewis thought danger was around, he dithered and worried and expected terrible things to happen before anything really began. He cleared his throat and said, "Hey, that's all right, Rose Rita. I like your stories."

"I'll remember that when I'm a famous writer," she mumbled. "Well, let's go. No use putting it off anymore."

They rode over to Mansion Street. "Mom!" Rose Rita yelled as they went inside. "Hey, Mom!"

There was no answer. The house had that deserted feeling that houses get when no one is around. They went into the kitchen. There on the counter beside the refrigerator was a cookie jar in the shape of a fat, laughing clown, and under the cookie jar was a sheet of blue-lined notebook paper. Rose Rita pulled it out and read it. "Oh, no," she groaned. "Now what are we gonna do?"

Lewis took the note from her and read it:

> *Dear Rosie,*
> *I may not be back until late, so please have your*
> *father's dinner heated up for him. The leftover meat*
> *loaf is in the refrigerator, and you can open a can of*
> *something. That wonderful Mr. Vanderhelm called*
> *me today. Someone told him that I sing in the*
> *church choir, and he says he has just the role for me*
> *in his grandfather's opera. I agreed to come and try*
> *out, and I may be gone for awhile. Imagine me right*
> *up there on stage! Of course he may not like my*
> *voice after he hears me, but it's thrilling just to be*
> *asked. Wish me luck, dear.*

The note was signed, "Love, Mother." Lewis let the paper fall from his numb fingers. "He knows about us," he told Rose Rita, fighting down the urge to scream. "That's why he called your mom, because we've been out looking for help. He's making sure we can't do anything to stop him!"

For a moment the two looked helplessly at each other. Then they both burst into frightened tears.

# CHAPTER EIGHT

"Here they are," said Lewis. He pulled a half-dozen large volumes from the special shelf where Jonathan Barnavelt kept his collection of magical books. Lewis had given his word that he would not disturb them, but this was an emergency; and anyway, the ones Lewis was taking weren't really about magic. They were tall, thick, clothbound books, made up of typewritten pages held together by inch-long brads that fastened the pages to the green covers. On the front of each book was a round gilt emblem with an Aladdin's lamp in the center. Stamped below it were the words TRANSACTIONS OF THE CAPHARNAUM COUNTY MAGICIANS SOCIETY. Beneath was a pair of dates. The first volume covered 1859–1880, the second one 1881–1900, and so on.

Lewis opened the volume dated 1918–1927. His uncle had showed him a couple of entries in these books before. They were mostly just records of the meetings. Lewis had seen an entry from 1932 that recorded Jonathan Barnavelt's admission to the society after he had successfully eclipsed the moon. Jonathan had also shown him one from 1922 that announced Mrs. Zimmermann's return from Europe with her husband, Honus. Now Lewis and Rose Rita were looking for something that might be a clue to what they were fighting.

Their earlier crying spell had not lasted long. Standing in her kitchen, Rose Rita got angry. "I am *not* going to let old Vanderhelm win," she vowed. "Magic music and magic statues, and no matter what else he has on his side, we're going to fight him. Now let's think up something we can do."

They stood side by side staring at the yellowing pages of the Magicians Society records. "This is hard," complained Rose Rita. "It's just a carbon copy, and it's old and smudged and I can barely read it."

Lewis switched on the desk lamp. The ancient print had faded to a pale gray, so it was like trying to read through foggy glass. "Let's just look for any mention of Vanderhelm," he said. He turned the fragile pages and the two friends read.

Most of what they found was ordinary stuff about elections and charity work. But then they came to May 1919, and the name "Vanderhelm" seemed to jump off the page at them. They both leaned down and bumped heads so hard that Lewis saw stars. "Ow!" he yelped. "Hey, cut it out. This is my uncle's book. You sit down and I'll read it to you."

Rubbing her forehead and scowling, Rose Rita seated herself in a comfortable green armchair. Lewis settled into his uncle's desk chair and read silently through several pages, ignoring Rose Rita's repeated pleas of "Come on! What's it say?"

Finally he whistled and looked up with frightened eyes. "This is awful," he said in an unsteady voice.

"What *is* it?" Rose Rita said. "Lewis Barnavelt, if you don't tell me this second, I'll never be your friend again as long as I live!"

"Okay," said Lewis. "Well, Immanuel Vanderhelm came to New Zebedee back in the winter of 1918, but nobody paid much attention to him. He was quiet, and also the whole town was down with a flu epidemic, just like your grandfather told us, and I guess most people were too miserable to care. But in April or May of 1919, he announced that he had written this opera and wanted to direct it. So the townspeople began to try out for it, just like they're doing now. Then the theater manager, Mr. Finster, came to see Mr. Mickleberry. This part was written by Mr. Mickleberry himself. Here, I'll read it out loud."

Lewis flipped back a couple of leaves and then began:

> *Mr. Finster knew that my stage magic was not all illusion, and he came to me for advice. He told me that he had a "feeling" that Immanuel Vanderhelm*

*was not what he seemed. I agreed to meet the man and see what I thought.*

*We met for lunch at Schuyler's Restaurant. I shall never forget the shock of seeing that sinister man. I tried St. Aloysius' Sigil of Revelation, but he countered with some diabolical spell of concealment, and I could learn nothing. However, our meeting proved to me that Vanderhelm was a powerful and evil wizard.*

*Later, by ways too tedious to detail here, I determined that Vanderhelm had gathered the necessary materials to create a simulacrum of the living, though I cannot understand why he would do such a thing. However, the worst came when Mr. Finster showed me some pages of the opera. It was clearly a magical incantation, and one so complex that it would require many voices to complete. Then I knew that the performance was a sham. Vanderhelm had recovered the ghastly necromantic spell that John Dee mentions as "The Incantation of Unbinding the Dead." He meant to trick the people of New Zebedee into singing this diabolical magical spell, and then he would become King of the Dead. Soon after I learned this, Mr. Finster disappeared (and I dread to think what has been done to him).*

Lewis looked up. Rose Rita was frowning. " 'King of the Dead,' " she repeated slowly. "Wasn't that what the ghost said?"

Lewis nodded. "I won't read it all, but the magicians got together and surrounded the theater when Immanuel

Vanderhelm was there alone. Mr. Mickleberry went in to see him. There was some kind of wizard's duel between them. This doesn't go into any details, but at the end everyone thought Vanderhelm was dead. To be safe, the society persuaded the town to close the theater. Some things aren't explained. For instance, nobody ever found Mr. Finster or learned what had happened to him."

"Does it give the spell the good magicians used?" asked Rose Rita.

"No," replied Lewis. "And what good would it do? We're not magicians. And this time Henry Vanderhelm has taken care of all the good magicians in town first."

Rose Rita's glare was teary behind her spectacles. "You think rotten old Vanderhelm has us licked, don't you? Well, I don't! I don't know how, but I'm going to save Mom from his clutches, and keep him from conducting his creepy old opera, and ch-chase him out of town—" She broke off and began to cry.

Lewis had a helpless, wretched sensation of dread. "Maybe we can do something," he muttered. "There has to be some way."

Rose Rita blew her nose. "What time is it?" she mumbled.

Lewis looked at his watch. "Five after three."

"I have to go home," Rose Rita said. "Mom asked me to make Dad's dinner, and he'll be home at four. You want to ride over with me?" When Lewis hesitated, Rose Rita almost pleaded: "After what happened in the cemetery, I'm scared. Please."

"Okay," said Lewis, but his heart was in his shoes. If Rose Rita was afraid, where did that leave him? Rose Rita was the brave one. He was just a worrywart. He got on his bike and rode beside Rose Rita down to Mansion Street.

When he returned, Mrs. Holtz still wasn't home, which was unusual. Normally she would not spend more than an hour or so shopping. Lewis tried the radio again, but just as he expected, he could only pick up WNZB.

He sat in the green armchair and tried hard to think of something to do. The study was warm and drowsy, and before he knew it, Lewis drifted into an exhausted sleep. He woke with a start hours later and saw that night had fallen. Edgy and afraid, he left the study and went looking for Mrs. Holtz. She still was not home, and by now she should have been cooking dinner.

Lewis called Rose Rita and told her that he was all alone. "Dad's home," she said, "but Mom's still at the stupid audition. You want to come over here?"

"Okay," Lewis said. Anything was better than sitting in the huge old Barnavelt house all by himself, jumping at every creak of wood or whisper of wind. He got his coat and went out front. Just as he was wheeling his bike down to the street, he heard a woman laughing.

Lewis squinted into the darkness. There was a streetlight between his house and Mrs. Zimmermann's next door, and the next light was a couple of houses away, each one casting a little yellowish island of illumination under it, leaving everything else dark. Two people walked into the cone of light down the street, and Lewis gasped as he recognized them. One was Mrs. Holtz, and the other was Henry Vanderhelm.

"Well," said Vanderhelm as the two came close to him. "Are you going on a little nocturnal expedition, my boy?"

"Lewis!" exclaimed Mrs. Holtz. "What are you thinking of? You get right back into the house this instant. You'll catch your death of cold out on a night like this, and then what will I tell your uncle Jonathan?"

Henry Vanderhelm laughed smoothly. "Oh, I wouldn't worry about Uncle Jonathan," he said. Lewis realized that Vanderhelm was talking to him, though the man seemed to be addressing Mrs. Holtz. "No, I shouldn't think Uncle Jonathan would be much to worry about. But you're right, Hannah. Lewis should go in. It seems to be a clear night, but these cold evenings can get foggy so very quickly. And he'll freeze like a stone statue."

"Goodness," said Mrs. Holtz. "I had no idea we'd been rehearsing so long. Good-bye, Mr. Vanderhelm, and thank you for putting me in the chorus. I know it's just a small part, but—"

"Tut, tut," said Vanderhelm. "In a work like my illustrious ancestor's, no part is small. Good evening, Hannah." He bowed and said to Lewis, "Goodnight, young man. Sleep like a stone, and remember what a very great service you have done for me and my art. In a way, the whole opera is your fault."

"What an odd way of putting it," said Mrs. Holtz.

His heart was pounding so hard, Lewis was afraid it

would burst. He didn't think Vanderhelm's words were an odd way of putting it at all.

Something awful was going to happen in New Zebedee because of the opera that he had found.

Vanderhelm was right.

It *was* all his fault.

# CHAPTER NINE

The next few days were strange and unsettling. The eerie fog that cut off New Zebedee from the rest of the world never lifted or thinned. The grocery stores ran out of things like fresh bread and milk. No out-of-town mail or newspapers or magazines showed up in New Zebedee. The television sets transmitted only static and snow, and the radios only picked up the New Zebedee station.

Yet to Lewis the scariest part was that no adult seemed to notice or care. Almost every family in town had someone involved in the opera, and all those families had become distracted and enchanted by the rehearsals. The opera would run about an hour and a half when it was all put together, Mrs. Pottinger told Rose Rita, but until the opening night the cast was rehearsing only half-hour segments at a time. New Zebedee was holding its breath, and even the people who were not involved with the opera were expecting it to mean great things for the town.

That included Rose Rita's father. He grumbled a little about how everything had come to a stop in town while the opera was being rehearsed. Still, he wound up saying, "Well, it'll be good for the place to have a little life in it, I suppose." Rose Rita didn't have the heart to argue with him.

She and Lewis saw a lot of each other, because the schools were not in session. Many of the teachers were in the opera, and Vanderhelm insisted that everyone in the cast rehearse for hours each day, from late morning into the night. Most of the kids took advantage of their unexpected break, but Lewis and Rose Rita moped around, trying to think of something new that might stop Vanderhelm's scheme. "We should be able to come up with *something*," groaned Rose Rita one afternoon. She and Lewis were in Jonathan's study again. "I mean, this isn't the first time you had to fight an evil spell."

Lewis shuddered at the memory that Rose Rita's words awakened. Years ago, when he first came to live with Uncle Jonathan, this very house had a dangerous magical item hidden inside it: a Doomsday Clock. The wicked sorcerer Isaac Izard had placed it there, and the ghost of Izard's wife had almost succeeded in activating it. Rose Rita had heard Lewis tell about the adventure, and about how Uncle Jonathan, Mrs. Zimmermann, and he had narrowedly averted the end of the world.

Things had changed since then. He was older and

more cautious about meddling with forces he did not understand. The house itself had been altered: Uncle Jonathan had ripped out all the old wallpaper, which had Isaac Izard's initials in it, and had replaced it with a more cheerful pattern. He had even exorcised the house of all evil influences. However, Henry Vanderhelm seemed to be at least as great a threat as the Izards had been. And most important, this time Lewis and Rose Rita were alone, without the help of good magicians. Lewis said so, and Rose Rita sighed.

"Maybe he overlooked one," she said.

Lewis scowled at her. "We tried every telephone number," he reminded her. "None of them is working. And every address we tried is a vacant lot, remember?"

"I know, I know," said Rose Rita. She pushed her black-rimmed glasses up on her nose and frowned. "There must be something old Vanderhelm forgot. He can't be everywhere at once. Hmm. Maybe the fog doesn't go up very high in the air. I wonder if you could fly out of New Zebedee?"

"Oh, sure," replied Lewis in a mocking voice. "I'll just tie on my cape and flap my arms and leap over the fog in a single bound, like Superman."

Rose Rita gave him a nasty look. "I didn't mean that you *personally* could fly out," she said. "But what about a—a balloon, maybe? Or a carrier pigeon?"

"Where do we get one?" asked Lewis. "I guess we might make a kite or something, but there's nowhere in town to buy a helium balloon or a carrier pigeon. Or do you want to try to catch one of the pigeons that roosts on the Civil War Monument?"

"No," said Rose Rita, "because where would he go? Just back to the monument, probably. Carrier pigeons have to be trained. Hmm. We could make a kite, but so what? Even if we got it out past the fog, it would probably just crash into a tree or something, and no one would pay any attention to it. I wish there was a magician left in town."

"There's no use wishing for that," grumped Lewis. "Vanderhelm took care of every one of them."

Suddenly Rose Rita sat up straighter in the chair. "Hold on! What about that Mildred Whosis?"

"Huh?" asked Lewis. "I don't know what you're talking about."

"Mildred Somebody-or-other!" insisted Rose Rita. "Mrs. Zimmermann was talking about her, remember? The one who couldn't get her spells to work out right? What was her name?"

Lewis had been sitting at Uncle Jonathan's desk, slumped forward. He straightened up too. "Right," he said. "It was a funny name. Not Johnson or Jackson. It started with a *J*, though. Uh—Jaeger, that was it! Mildred Jaeger!"

Rose Rita jumped up and grabbed the address book on the desk. She flipped through it hurriedly. "She isn't here!" Rose Rita announced. "So she isn't a member of the Magicians Society."

Lewis dug out the skinny New Zebedee telephone

book and turned to the *J*'s. "Here she is," he said. "Mildred Sherman Jaeger. She lives over on Marshall Street." He reached for the phone and when the operator came on the line, he asked for Mildred Jaeger's number. Lewis held his breath. The phone rang once . . . twice . . . three times—

"Hello?" It was a friendly voice, an elderly voice.

"Uh, hello, Mrs. Jaeger?" Lewis stammered.

"Yes. Who is calling, please?"

Lewis clamped his hand over the receiver and looked at Rose Rita for help. "What do I tell her?" he whispered.

"Tell her who you are," Rose Rita shot back. "Ask her if we can come and see her."

Lewis swallowed. "Uh, Mrs. Jaeger, you don't know me, but my name is Lewis Barnavelt. My uncle is Jonathan Barnavelt."

"Oh, dear me, yes," said the cheerful voice. "Dear Jonathan, such a thoughtful man. How is he?"

"He's not in town right now," replied Lewis. "Do you remember Lucius Mickleberry?"

"Oh, of course. I knew him quite well when he lived in New Zebedee."

Hurriedly, Lewis told Mrs. Jaeger about the mission his uncle had undertaken. Then he said, "Mrs. Jaeger, have you noticed something odd about the town lately?"

"It has been very quiet," admitted Mrs. Jaeger.

"Well, we think that something terrible is going on, and we need to talk to someone who knows about—" Lewis dropped his voice almost to a whisper—"magic."

There was such a long pause that Lewis was afraid the woman had hung up. Finally, though, she said, "Dear, I wish I could help, but perhaps you should get in touch with some other people. There is a Magicians Society in town."

"We can't talk to them," said Lewis, and in a rush he explained why.

After another long silence Mrs. Jaeger said, "I think perhaps you had better come over, dear. I don't know what I can do, but I'll help in any way I can. Do you know how to get to my house?" She gave him directions.

Lewis said good-bye to her, and he and Rose Rita ran out to their bikes. It was a day of pale, watery sunlight, with everything looking cold and dead, and the air seemed stagnant and lifeless as they pedaled toward Marshall Street.

Mrs. Jaeger's house was a one-story cottage on a block of modest little homes. Rose Rita and Lewis climbed off their bikes and rang the doorbell, and Lewis nervously scraped his shoes on the welcome mat as they waited for someone to answer the door. After a moment the door swung open and they found themselves facing a short, plump gray-haired woman. Her hair was in a bun, and she was wearing a blue dress and a frilly white apron. Her blue eyes looked huge behind gold-rimmed spectacles. "Come in, come in," she said, waving the two friends inside. "I was just making some lunch. Do you care for chicken soup? It's homemade, and I have some lovely fresh bread I just baked this morning."

Lewis was ravenous, and Rose Rita said she was hungry too. Mrs. Jaeger refused to hear a word of their story until they each had a generous bowl of hot delicious soup, with toasted homemade bread and steaming cups of cocoa. The meal warmed Lewis and made him feel more like his normal self than he had in awhile. Mrs. Holtz had almost stopped cooking anything except canned goods, and Lewis missed her hearty meals.

"Now," said Mrs. Jaeger, "tell me about this trouble."

She listened while Lewis told her about Vanderhelm and the opera, with Rose Rita adding facts here and there when Lewis forgot something important. Mrs. Jaeger's magnified eyes grew rounder and more solemn, and she shook her head dolefully. "My, my," she said when Lewis and Rose Rita had finished. "This is very bad. Much worse than I thought. I should have noticed all this myself, but I never listen to the radio, and I don't subscribe to any out-of-town newspapers. Still, the air has been full of bad feelings. I just put it down to growing old and arthritic."

"Can you help us?" asked Rose Rita.

Mrs. Jaeger bit her lip. "I don't know, dear. Of course I do remember old Vanderhelm. I was just a young woman then, but I was still trying to become a member of the Magicians Society. I'm afraid I wasn't much good as a sorceress. Since then I've learned that I *am* very good at making cherry preserves and stitching quilts and cooking. I believe you should always do what you are best at, and so I've given up magic."

"Tell us about old Vanderhelm," said Lewis. "We

don't know anything about what he was up to, or how the Magicians Society defeated him."

"Well, I'm not sure I know much about that myself, dear." Mrs. Jaeger sipped her cocoa. "I remember this much: Mr. Vanderhelm's spell was a terribly hard and complex one. It was so powerful that one person could not speak it alone. That is why he wrote the opera. If all the actors sang the lyrics in the right order, then the opera itself became his spell. With that many voices, it would work."

"What would it do?" asked Rose Rita.

Mrs. Jaeger sighed. "I don't want to frighten you children."

"Don't worry about that," Lewis assured her. "We're plenty scared already!"

"Well—" The woman's face looked troubled. At last, though, she said, "As I understood it, the spell would awaken all the dead sorcerers from the past. Their spirits would come in answer to the summons, and Vanderhelm would enable them to possess the bodies of the living. Then they would be his slaves. He would be the King of the Dead, with an army of incredibly potent magicians to do his bidding. With that kind of power, it would be a simple thing for him to take over the whole world. He would be the dictator of the entire human race."

Lewis shook, remembering Henry Vanderhelm's cunning voice and oily manner. A world ruled by such a person would not be a pleasant place.

Rose Rita said, "Is that all?"

"I am afraid not," said Mrs. Jaeger. "With the power the spell would give him, Vanderhelm could also command the ordinary, unmagical dead. Their bodies would rise from their tombs and march to his orders. He would have a whole army of the dead to do his bidding—and the dead greatly outnumber the living. If anyone dared to oppose him, Vanderhelm would simply have that person killed, and in death the person would become just another one of Vanderhelm's servants."

"That's awful," said Rose Rita, her voice trembling. "Isn't there anything anyone can do?"

"Well, there are some safeguards," said Mrs. Jaeger. "The spell will not work if anyone has shed blood, for example, so Vanderhelm could not just kill anyone who tried to oppose him. Of course, after the spell is complete he can kill whomever he wants. But bad magic can always be counteracted with good. That is how the Magicians Society defeated him. They put together a spell of their own that protected them and prevented him from enchanting all the people in town. Then Lucius Mickleberry confronted him in a duel and defeated him. You see, a bad magician seldom has many friends to help with his or her evil spells, and there is strength in numbers."

"That might have worked back in 1919, but what can *we* do?" asked Lewis. "Somehow or other Henry Vanderhelm has put a spell on all the magicians in New Zebedee except you. We can't act together with all of them, because they're all missing. Can you fight him?"

Mrs. Jaeger sighed deeply. "I wasn't any good as a

magician," she said in a small voice. "I tried and tried, but every spell I cast went wrong or backfired. Oh, Lewis, I'm sure that your uncle or maybe Florence Zimmermann could fight this new Vanderhelm, but I am rusty and out of practice and not very talented besides."

"Then it's hopeless?" asked Rose Rita.

"Of course not!" returned Mrs. Jaeger in a brisk voice. "That's nonsense. Nothing is ever hopeless. We will simply have to put our heads together and come up with something that might help us. I only wish," she added regretfully, "that I had some idea of what that might be."

# CHAPTER TEN

They stayed at Mrs. Jaeger's house for hours. She had Lewis climb up a rickety ladder into the attic and bring down a small suitcase, which she opened in her living room. Rose Rita and Lewis sat side by side on a soft sofa embroidered with pink roses and green leaves, and Mrs. Jaeger knelt in front of her coffee table. She took a half-finished jigsaw puzzle off the table and put it away in its box. The cover showed that the puzzle was a colorful scene of picnickers in a field full of daisies, tiger lilies, and primroses, with a red barn and silo and a herd of black-and-white Holstein cows in the background.

"I'm afraid I haven't had these things out in twenty years or more," apologized Mrs. Jaeger. "I hope the moths haven't gotten at them." The sharp odor of naphtha rose from inside the suitcase. Lewis and Rose Rita leaned forward as Mrs. Jaeger pulled out a long wooden spoon, an ancient book bound in crumbling black leather, a white satin robe, and small jars wrapped in old newspaper. "My wand," said Mrs. Jaeger, waving the spoon about.

Rose Rita and Lewis looked at each other.

Mrs. Jaeger sighed. "Oh, I know that magicians are supposed to have hazelwood wands or ebony staves or silver scepters, but none of those things ever appealed to me. I've always loved to cook, so when the time came for me to enchant a wand, I chose the object that seemed best for me."

"That's all right," said Rose Rita. "After all, Mrs. Zimmermann's wand is a plain black umbrella."

"That's true!" agreed Mrs. Jaeger with a happy smile. "And Lewis, your uncle chose a walking stick, if I remember correctly. Well, this is what I chose, and it always worked. Uh, sort of." She tapped her chin with the spoon. "Hmm. Let me see. What do you think we should try? I'm afraid that I simply don't have enough power to fight this new Vanderhelm successfully."

"Could you get in touch with another magician?" asked Lewis. "One who might be, well—"

"Better at this than I am?" asked Mrs. Jaeger with a smile. "Don't worry, dear, you won't embarrass me. Yes, that is a good idea. In fact, let's see if we can conjure up some way to speak to your uncle, Lewis."

Following Mrs. Jaeger's instructions, Lewis brought a glass of water from the kitchen. "Put that on the coffee table," Mrs. Jaeger told him. "We'll try to use it like a scrying glass or crystal ball. If we're lucky, we'll at least get your uncle's image—and maybe his attention."

Then Mrs. Jaeger wriggled into her satin gown, which was cut like a choir robe and had become rather tight, and began to wave her spoon over the glass. She chanted something in ancient Chaldean, then in Coptic, and finally in Old High German. At last she waved the spoon commandingly and said in English, "One, two, three, wherever they may be, let Florence Zimmermann or Jonathan Barnavelt see and speak with me!"

A goldfish appeared in the glass. It looked somewhat startled, and then it settled down to swimming round and round in tight little circles.

"Oh, dear," said Mrs. Jaeger. "I still don't seem to have the knack."

Lewis had been holding his breath, and now let it whoosh out. Mrs. Jaeger had half scared him into thinking that maybe the fish *was* Uncle Jonathan, but it looked like an ordinary Woolworth's pet-department goldfish, not magical at all.

"It's getting dark," Rose Rita said.

Mrs. Jaeger shook her head. "Well, perhaps you children had better go home. I will think about this and try to figure out what went wrong. Maybe I left some words out, or maybe my pronunciation isn't quite right. I'll call you tomorrow if I can come up with anything. Do either of you have goldfish?"

"No," said Rose Rita and Lewis together.

"Hmm. Then I suppose I'll have to find a bowl for

this one. And I'll need a good fishy name. Dear me, so much to think about!"

"Uh, Mrs. Jaeger?" asked Lewis hesitantly. "Will you be in any danger? I mean, Henry Vanderhelm has done something to all the other magicians in New Zebedee. Will he come after you now?"

"Bless you, dear, I don't think so," replied Mrs. Jaeger. "My magic hardly disturbs the flow, you see, so he probably won't feel it. And whatever spell he worked to put all the others out of commission must have been done all at once. My guess is that he got hold of a list of the Capharnaum County Magicians Society, and he cast a spell over everyone whose name appeared in it. I think your uncle and Florence Zimmermann were probably out of range in Florida. Anyway, if he tried to add me to the list now, he'd probably find that something would go wrong. One of the hardest things in the world is to change a spell that has already started. So I believe I am safe. After all, I'm not much of a threat, am I?"

Lewis had to agree that she was not. He and Rose Rita said good-bye, and they pedaled back to Mansion Street in the gathering dusk. Lewis waited until Rose Rita had gone inside, and then he started home, wishing that he had a bike light that worked. Clouds had gathered as the sun went down, and now it was getting dark fast. He was huffing and puffing up the hill when he heard something behind him.

Fearfully, Lewis glanced back over his shoulder. He saw a light behind him, faint and indistinct. He swerved toward the curb, thinking that a car was closing in on him and wanting to pass. Then he heard a dismal wailing howl, so startling that he jerked the front wheel of his bike against the curb.

*Crash!* The bike banged to the pavement, and Lewis went flying through the air, turning somersaults. He hardly had time to be scared. *Thud!* He hit the sidewalk flat on his back, chuffing the breath out of him. With the concrete cold and hard beneath him, he lay there trying to breathe, but his lungs would not work. He felt a rising panic. Finally, after what seemed like an hour, he managed a wheezy gasp, and air rushed into his burning chest. He was dizzy and nauseated, but he tried to get up. Rolling to his stomach, he pushed himself up on his hands and knees.

The light was closer now, but it was no car. Lewis squinted. A wavery, pale white glow spread across the whole street, and it was silently coming closer and closer. It seemed to bob up and down. What in the world could it be? He did not want to stay around to find out. He scrambled to his bike, pulled it upright, swung up onto the seat, and pushed himself off.

The bike wobbled because he was trying to pedal it uphill, but it did not fall over. Lewis forced the pedals down, but he could not gain much speed. The wheels barely moved.

And the glow caught up with him. A sickly wave of cold air washed over Lewis, making his teeth chatter. He blinked. He found himself in the middle of a row of human figures, gaunt and hollow-eyed and skeletal. They reached for him with long, bony fingers, and their bony jaws dropped open in yawning grins of welcome, and their bony legs trailed behind, their feet not even touching the ground. He was in a cloud of ghosts!

"Beware!" one of them breathed, its skull face inches away. The teeth snapped at Lewis, making him wince. He turned the bike, desperately plunging down the hill. Icy fingers caressed his face and plucked at his coat as the bike picked up speed. One of the ghosts was holding onto Lewis's right arm, trying to jerk it and make Lewis hit the curb again. Lewis could feel the tugs like sudden gusts of wind, but they were not strong enough to pull him off balance.

"Get away!" shrieked Lewis. He had left most of the ghostly figures behind, but at least two clung to him, the one on his arm and the one whose grip he could feel on the collar and back of his coat.

"Join us," hissed an evil voice right in his ear. "Sleep the long sleep!"

"Be his," whispered the phantom holding onto Lewis's arm. "It is useless to resist him."

"It's dark in the grave," the other said, its voice dry and raspy like a rush of dead leaves on a Halloween-night wind. "Dark and tight and silent!"

"Give up, give up," the phantom chanted. "Be his servant!"

Lewis thought he really was about to die. He hurtled down the hill faster than he had ever dared ride even in the daytime. He did not stop or slow down, because he had the horrible feeling that these ghostly creatures would seize him and hold him until their friends came —and then what? Would they carry him away? Pull him down into a tomb? *Make him one of them?*

Main Street flashed by, and Lewis almost fell as his bike racketed over the railroad tracks. "No!" howled one of the ghosts. Its hands tried to tear at his face in fury, but the hooked claws slipped over his skin like drops of icy water. The bike plunged into the unearthly fog.

"We're fading!" screeched one of the voices. "Fading into the fog. . . ." The voice became higher and higher, until its dying wail hung on like the whine of a pesky mosquito, and then even that died away.

Lewis was crying. He stopped his bike and stood on his right leg, his chest heaving and his heart hammering. He had lost the terrible creatures by blundering into the fog that surrounded the town—but had he also lost himself?

He gathered all his courage, dismounted from his bike, and rolled it forward. The fog clung to him with cold, clammy tendrils. Everything was a horrible gray-black, as if Lewis were floating in a vast nothingness. What if he could not find the way back? Would he be doomed to wander this foggy netherworld until he died? What if something awful, like the ghastly living statue, were stalking him in the murk?

Just then he saw a smear of red light ahead. He rolled his bike across the railroad tracks, and right ahead was a stoplight, uselessly changing from red to green. Lewis almost screamed with relief. The town slept. He saw no ghosts.

Still, he took the long way home, frantically pedaling to the summit of High Street. He let his bike crash to the ground as soon as he was inside the wrought-iron gate, and he ran stumbling up the front steps. Lewis charged through the front door and slammed it behind him. He stood with his back against the door, holding it shut, trying to keep out the ghosts.

"Lewis?" It was Mrs. Holtz. She came frowning into the foyer. "What on earth?"

"He really is staying out too late," came a silky voice from behind her. "Hannah, I imagine his uncle would approve if you kept the boy inside."

Lewis almost passed out. The horrible Mr. Henry Vanderhelm was right here, inside his uncle's house! He came up behind Mrs. Holtz and stood smiling at Lewis, but there was nothing friendly in that smile.

"Yes-s-s," said Mrs. Holtz thoughtfully. "I believe you are right. Lewis, I am sorry, but since you never seem to let me know where you are going, you will simply have to stay here in the house until your uncle returns home."

"Oh, let's not be too hard," purred Vanderhelm. "Let's say that Lewis will be permitted to see the performance. I think that is only fitting."

"But Mr. Barnavelt will be home by then," protested Mrs. Holtz.

"Perhaps," said Vanderhelm. "Perhaps not. At any rate, I can promise our young friend that it will be something to see! Lewis, my boy, I have no doubt you soon will be one of us—an opera lover—forever."

Lewis could take the strain no longer. He did not scream. He did not even try to run.

He fainted dead away.

# CHAPTER ELEVEN

Lewis woke up in his own room. Everything was quiet and dark. He jerked to a sitting position and clicked on the bedside lamp. Everything seemed normal. The Westclox ticked away showing the time as 1:15. Then Lewis caught sight of himself in the tall mirror near the fireplace. His blond hair was disheveled like a crazy mop, and his round face stared back pale and frightened. He had been lying on the covers with a blanket thrown over him. Someone—was it the horrible Mr. Vanderhelm?— had carried Lewis into the room and had placed him on the bed, fully clothed except for his shoes. Lewis got up and locked his bedroom door. He went to the window and looked out. He could see the Hanchett house, shadowy and asleep across the street, and the dim form of the water tower at the top of the hill. Only the street lights made little splashes of weak yellow light here and there.

Lewis undressed and crept back into bed. He lay cowering beneath the covers for a long time, shivering and whispering prayers he had learned as an altar boy. He had the disturbing feeling that he would never sleep again, but somehow he finally fell into an exhausted slumber. In baleful dreams he ran again and again from those eerie, clinging, clammy ghosts, but he did not wake until daylight streamed in through his window. As he climbed wearily out of bed, he heard something rustle beneath his pillow. Frowning, he fumbled for it and pulled out a folded sheet of thick, heavy paper. He opened it and read a message written in a slashing handwriting in black letters that looked as if they had been cut into the page:

> *Boy,*
> *Cease your foolish struggle against me. My servants are everywhere. If you go out again before the great night, you will pay the most horrible penalty.*
> *You have been warned.*

Lewis began to shake. He was marked for a grisly fate, and he knew no way of avoiding it. To someone with Lewis's imagination, a vague phrase like "the most horrible penalty" conjured up all sorts of anguish and suffering. He dressed and slipped downstairs on trembling legs. Every shadow and every sound made him jump, even though he was in his own house. A sense of shame almost crushed him. Lewis was sure he was the worst coward alive. Oh, sure, he had summoned up false bravado at times, like when he pretended he was Sherlock Holmes or when he was with someone really brave like Rose Rita or his English pen pal, Bertie Goodring. When the chips were down, though, and when he had to face the unknown alone, he was a quivering wreck.

Mrs. Holtz had already left, so Lewis got his own breakfast of Cheerios and toast. The cereal stuck in a thick lump in his throat, and he had to struggle to swallow. What was he to do? The sun was shining brightly outside, but Lewis was too terrified to go into the front yard. He was afraid even to pick up the phone. If he called Rose Rita, would Vanderhelm's servants discover the call and come for him?

Lewis thought back to the bad time when the house was under the spell of Isaac Izard. Uncle Jonathan, Mrs. Zimmermann, and Lewis had finally discovered the hiding place of the Doomsday Clock in a wacky way when Lewis made up a crazy magic spell. He wondered if he could do it again. True, Jonathan and Mrs. Zimmermann were not here, so he could not call on their magic. Still, Mrs. Zimmermann had said that New Zebedee had lots of magic flowing through it. Lewis gritted his teeth and decided he had to try. He went into the study, pulled out a pad and pencil, and spent some time working up the craziest ritual he could devise. Whatever happened, it might give them a clue to defeating Vanderhelm.

When the ratchety old mechanical doorbell growled at twenty minutes to twelve, Lewis was still seated at his uncle's desk. The sound nearly made him jump out of his skin. He grabbed a couple of books and covered the notes he had been making, then pushed the chair back from the desk and hurried to the front hall. The bell rang again. As Lewis was getting up the nerve to ask, "Who's there?" a familiar voice called out, "Hey, Lewis! Are you at home?"

It was Rose Rita. With a relieved sigh, Lewis opened the door. Rose Rita stood there, dressed in her P.F. Flyers tennis shoes, long black socks, a red-and-green plaid wool skirt, and her father's old University of Michigan letter jacket. She wore a knitted green cap on her head, which she clapped down with one hand. Behind Rose Rita was Mrs. Jaeger, bundled into a heavy long gray coat and a furry hat. The day was bright, with a blustery wind. "About time," grumped Rose Rita. "We almost blew away out here." She pushed past Lewis, and he stood aside to let Mrs. Jaeger in. Then he closed the door and locked it.

"Hey," he said. "With wind blowing like that, maybe the fog—"

"No such luck," said Rose Rita, shucking off her jacket. "I checked. It's hanging there as calm as curtains, even with all that wind."

"It's magical, I expect," said Mrs. Jaeger as Lewis helped her out of her coat. "This wind just blows right through it without disturbing it in the least."

Rose Rita started to hang her jacket and hat on the coat rack. "Yeah," she said. "I don't know if—hey! Why didn't you tell me about this?" She pointed at the mirror.

Lewis gasped. The mirror showed Uncle Jonathan's face. He was brushing his teeth. "Hey!" Lewis shouted, waving his arms wildly. "Uncle Jonathan!"

Too late. Uncle Jonathan spat into an unseen sink and turned away. The vision shimmered and faded and the mirror was just a mirror again.

"Oh, my," said Mrs. Jaeger. "I believe my magic spell worked, after all. That was a vision of your uncle, sure enough."

"I don't know," said Lewis. "I saw an image of Uncle Jonathan and Mrs. Zimmermann there once before."

Mrs. Jaeger looked thoughtful. "Hmm. Since this mirror apparently knows how to show us Jonathan, it might be useful, with a little help."

"What kind of help?" asked Rose Rita.

"I believe Jonathan must have been facing a mirror on his end of the image. You usually do look in the mirror when you brush your teeth." Mrs. Jaeger pursed her lips in thought. "Next time, we could be ready. If we could work the right spell, whenever Jonathan is looking into a mirror, he would see anyone looking into this mirror at the same time. That is, if the person on this end concentrates hard and wills him to see. I'll try a little enchantment. Lewis, you will have to keep a close watch on this mirror."

"I will," replied Lewis in a miserable voice. "I can't believe we missed him by a second."

"It happens," sighed Mrs. Jaeger. "Magic is tricky and unpredictable. Believe me, I know. The goldfish is doing very well, by the way." She thought for another minute, chanted an incantation, and waved her spoon. "Maybe that will do it."

"Whether it does or not," Lewis said, "I'm glad you're here." Briefly he explained what he wanted to try. Mrs. Jaeger nodded and looked as if she were carefully thinking over what he told her. "So," he finished, "if this works, maybe we can get a better idea of what might break Vanderhelm's spell."

"Sounds screwy to me," said Rose Rita. When Lewis looked crestfallen, she grinned. "Hey, that doesn't matter. The whole business is screwy, anyway, so maybe it will work all the better. Let's try it."

Lewis went into the study and brought back his notes. Mrs. Jaeger read them, a smile flickering on her lips. Then she passed them to Rose Rita, who giggled aloud. "Boy," she said, "are we ever going to look like idiots! But let's try it. Is it okay if we stay here, so we can keep an eye on the mirror?"

"Sure," replied Lewis. "In fact, maybe all the spell will do is contact Uncle Jonathan. I won't know until we try it, anyway." He ran off to get the materials.

In a few minutes they were ready. Lewis set up the folding card table and brought in three chairs. They could hardly look at each other without laughing. Lewis had used poster paint to color his face half green and half yellow. Over his regular clothes he wore one of his uncle's nightshirts, a bright orange tent that billowed around him. Rose Rita had tied her hair up in two ponytails that stuck up from her head like antennae. She had turned her father's jacket inside out and wore her hat on her left foot and her left shoe on her left hand. Mrs. Jaeger had dusted her face with flour and had given herself a bright red clown nose with her lipstick. She had tied her magic spoon to a black string and wore it like a necklace. They all sat at the table holding hands.

"Now what?" asked Mrs. Jaeger. "Do we commune with the spirits, or go trick-or-treating?"

"No," answered Lewis. "Now we sing the mystical song until we get a sign that will help us."

"And what's the song?" asked Rose Rita.

" 'Row, Row, Row Your Boat,' " Lewis told her. "Except we have to sing it as a round, and when you finish it forwards, you have to sing it again backwards!"

It took them a number of tries to get it right, but finally each one was able to sing the words both ways. Rose Rita was a passable soprano, Mrs. Jaeger sang a slightly off-key alto, and Lewis tried to deliver a baritone. The third time they went through the round without a mistake, something happened. Lewis had just finished his backward run with "Stream the down gently boat your row, row, row," when all the clocks in the house struck thirteen at once.

It made quite a clamor. Uncle Jonathan no longer owned as many clocks as he once had, back when he was trying to drown out the ticking of the Doomsday Clock, but there were still a dozen clocks in the house, from the big old grandfather's clock down to Lewis's bedside

Westclox. Every clock made noise, even the ones that did not normally chime. When the last one had rung, the mirror on the hat stand flashed to life.

For a moment it flickered and blazed in different colors, pale blue, white, rosy pink. Then it shimmered into a black-and-white image, just like a TV picture. A serious-looking man sat at a desk reading from a sheet of paper. He wore a tall peaked wizard's hat with flashing moons and stars and planets on it, and he had a long white beard. "Hello out there in magic land," this man said in a deep voice. "It's time for the World Magic News. Dateline, New Zebedee, Michigan: Tomorrow evening Henry Vanderhelm will attempt to become King of the Dead by having his magic spell sung by the townspeople who have come under his spell. This disaster can be averted, but only by someone who knows the score. Henry Vanderhelm can be shown up for what he is— but it will be a dangerous chance! Please reflect on that, viewers." The mirror went dark.

The three friends sat looking at each other. "Well, that helped about as much as a tuna-fish sandwich helps a broken leg," grumbled Rose Rita.

"No, no," murmured Mrs. Jaeger. "It did help. Now we know when Mr. Vanderhelm will make his move. Maybe we can stop him, or at least slow him down."

"Slow him down," repeated Lewis. "Maybe we can at that. I wonder if we could do something to the theater?"

"Like what?" asked Rose Rita, struggling to take off her inside-out jacket. "Burn it down?"

"Not exactly," answered Lewis. "But what if the fire

sprinklers came on? Or what if all the musical instruments got sabotaged? That might give us some time."

"It's worth a try," said Rose Rita slowly. "But when can we do it?"

"It will have to be tonight," Mrs. Jaeger said. "After the rehearsal is over."

Lewis trembled with fear. He had not really thought his plan through before speaking. Now that he thought of going into that spooky theater in the dark, he felt ill and dizzy. It was the last thing he wanted to do.

But he knew he had to try.

# CHAPTER TWELVE

Jonathan Barnavelt had just finished brushing his teeth when he heard Mrs. Zimmermann call him from her room. He went down the hall and found the door open. Mrs. Zimmermann was sitting at the window, knitting a purple scarf and listening to the national news on the radio. Outside, the sunny Florida sky was blue and cloudless, but Mrs. Zimmermann was frowning. "What is it, Hag-Face?" asked Jonathan in a teasing voice. "Has—"

With a frown, Mrs. Zimmermann shushed him. "Listen," she said. "Just before the commercial, the announcer said a news story about New Zebedee was coming up."

The radio was playing the last few bars of an Ipana

toothpaste commercial. When it was over, the newscast continued.

A genial and good-natured voice said, "Has anyone found a small Michigan town? Because the United States Post Office and some other people are looking for one. According to the post office, its delivery trucks have not been able to find a town called New Zebedee for days now. Local farmers also report difficulty in getting to New Zebedee, and they blame their problems on an unseasonable fog. Better watch out—if the post office can manage to lose a whole town, just think what it could do with those tax-refund checks!"

The announcer went on to another news story. Mrs. Zimmermann put down her knitting and switched off the radio. "I think," she said, "it is time for us to go home."

For once Jonathan did not tease her. He nodded and said, "I'll go call the airport. Get packed. We'll fly to Detroit on the first available flight."

"Jonathan?" asked Mrs. Zimmermann.

"Yes, Florence?"

"Do you think the children are all right?"

"I was just going to call." Jonathan hurried away. He and Mrs. Zimmermann had already settled Lucius Mickleberry's estate, and they had planned to leave for home in two days. Three wooden crates held Mr. Mickleberry's books of magic and collection of amulets, and these were ready to be shipped back to New Zebedee. Jonathan tried long distance, only to be told that the lines to

New Zebedee had not been open for days. He called the airport, and after that a freight company. Then he hurried back to Mrs. Zimmermann's room.

She had pulled the window shade down and had closed the drapes. Her black umbrella was clasped in front of her, and the golf-ball-sized crystal orb that formed part of the handle glowed purple. The light shifted and pulsed, casting weird patterns that flowed and fluttered over the walls and over Mrs. Zimmermann's face. It looked like the flickering light seen underwater through a diving mask. Mrs. Zimmermann sighed and the glimmer faded.

"Anything?" asked Jonathan as Mrs. Zimmermann stood up and opened the curtains and the window shade.

"Nothing," she said. "Now I'm really worried. I don't often used the crystal as a scrying ball, but when I do, it never fails. If it can't show me New Zebedee, there must be some kind of magical barrier around the town." She opened the closet and took out her big suitcase, which she tossed on the bed. She opened it and began to take articles of clothing from drawers and pack them. "What did you find out?"

"Not much," Jonathan told her, and he explained that the phones were out.

"I don't like the sound of that," Mrs. Zimmermann said. "Did you call the airport?"

"We've just missed the last flight today. There's a plane at eight o'clock tomorrow morning that stops in Atlanta, Louisville, and Detroit," replied Jonathan. "It will get us to Detroit by four in the afternoon. We should be able to get to New Zebedee late tomorrow."

Mrs. Zimmermann had been folding a purple sweater. She put it in the suitcase and looked at Jonathan with haunted eyes. "I wish I knew what we will find there."

All Jonathan could do was shiver.

That very night, Rose Rita and Lewis crouched uncomfortably inside the doorway of the Farmers' Seed & Feed. Mrs. Jaeger was at her house, trying to come up with a magic spell that might help them thwart or delay Vanderhelm's plan. Lewis and Rose Rita were going to try to throw a monkey wrench into the works at the theater. Huddling in the cold doorway, they heard the distant sounds of music and many voices joined together in song, often interrupted by long periods of silence. During one of these pauses, Rose Rita whispered, "I guess old Vanderhelm is giving them directions." Lewis did not reply.

Finally, about ten o'clock, people left in groups of three and four, some humming, some chatting together, a few silent. They saw Mrs. Holtz and Rose Rita's mother go by. When no one else came out, the two friends slipped out from their hiding place. Rose Rita tried the doorknob. "It's unlocked," she said. "Come on."

A dim light burned at the head of the stairs. Lewis followed Rose Rita, his pulse drumming wildly. The smell of fresh paint filled the air, and when they stepped out into the vestibule of the theater, Lewis gasped at the change that had taken place. The overhead lights burned, showing that the walls had been freshly painted, the thick red carpet thoroughly cleaned, and the whole place tidied up. It wasn't nearly as dilapidated and forbidding as it had been on their first visit. Rose Rita hurried to the auditorium. "It's dark in here," she announced. "Let's see if we can find the lights."

They searched for quite awhile before Lewis had the idea of going into the coat-check alcove. A doorway there led into a small booth with a window that looked out into the darkened auditorium. A single dim bulb burned here, illuminating a control panel covered with switches. "This must be the light booth," said Lewis. "But which of these do we throw?"

"Try them all," Rose Rita replied. She reached for the nearest switch and pulled it down. Immediately a rose-colored light bathed the right part of the stage.

Lewis threw some switches, and more stage lights came on. Finally he noticed one large switch off to the left. A label below it said *HOUSE* in capital letters. When he tried that switch, a chandelier high over the auditorium came on, and in its light Lewis could see the rows of seats, newly cleaned and mended. "Okay," said Rose Rita. "Let's see what we can do."

They went into the cavernous auditorium. Lewis's flesh crawled with distaste and fear. The place looked clean and neat, but it had a sinister atmosphere, as if someone were watching their every move. Suddenly something occurred to Lewis. "Hey," he said in a hoarse whisper, "did you see him?"

"See who?" asked Rose Rita in a irritable voice. They

had reached the stage, on which a series of backdrops depicted a small town. In the orchestra pit below, the brass instruments gleamed. Surprisingly, a scattering of sheet music lay all over the floor of the pit, as if the musicians had just carelessly tossed down their music when they had finished rehearsing. "See who?" asked Rose Rita again, glancing around. "I don't know who you mean."

"Vanderhelm," returned Lewis. "We saw about half the town come out of the building, but I didn't notice Vanderhelm. Did you?"

"He was probably in one of the groups," said Rose Rita with a shrug. "Hey, I've got an idea. Let's get all this music together and burn it. I'd like to see them try to do the opera with no music!"

Lewis hesitated. He remembered only too well the last time he had gone down into the orchestra pit. But Rose Rita was already descending the steps, so Lewis gritted his teeth and followed. "I don't like this place," he whispered.

Rose Rita put her hands on her hips. "Well, we won't be here long. What a mess! Here, help me." Stooping, she reached for a handful of the music, and Lewis bent to do the same.

*Whoosh!* A wind sprang up from nowhere, making Rose Rita shriek in alarm and Lewis leap backward. He stumbled against the steps and sat down hard on the second one from the bottom. Rose Rita backed toward him, the wind whipping her long hair all around her face. The sheet music rose up in the air, the cloud of papers billowing up, then spinning into a whirlwind. It rustled and fluttered as it settled into a cone of madly swirling paper as tall as a man. "Let's go," said Rose Rita, yanking Lewis to his feet.

She ran up the stairs, pulling Lewis, who stumbled up backward, unable to tear his gaze away from the amazing sight. The gusting sheet music grew more compact and took on the shape of a man. Then it *was* a man, a man made of paper, with a paper cloak billowing behind him, long paper arms reaching out toward Lewis, and a blank paper face turned blindly toward him. Its paper legs rustled as the incredible apparition took a step, and then the ink that made up the music notes flowed together into patterns of black and white. The paper man became a sketch of Vanderhelm. The black eyes glared, the black lips sneered, and at the ends of the tubular arms the ink flowed into long, grasping fingers. Another step, and the creature took on the colors of life, and the lips moved as Vanderhelm's voice boomed out: "Foolish children! I warned you once, and you get no second warning!"

The creature's strong hand closed on Lewis's flailing wrist. From the top of the stairs, Rose Rita tugged Lewis's shoulder, trying to drag him out into the auditorium. Vanderhelm, or the thing that looked like him, yanked harder. Lewis felt himself being pulled downward. "Run, Rose Rita!" he shrieked at the top of his lungs. Powerful hands clamped onto him, and he almost fainted. He heard Rose Rita's voice as if from a long way off: "I'll get help, Lewis!"

The hands lifted Lewis clear off the ground. The creature that had taken Vanderhelm's form was incredibly strong. Lewis dangled in its grasp like a rag doll. He thought he would die from sheer terror.

The cruel eyes looked into his. "I must not shed blood before the ritual is complete," muttered Vanderhelm. "So you may live for a little while. What to do with you in the meantime?" He paused, a crafty expression on his face. "Well, why not?" he muttered at last. "They never found the other one, the one my master hid away all those years ago, the one who caused trouble like you. Yes, I think that would be most fitting."

Lewis gasped as Vanderhelm tucked him under one arm and strode up the steps into the auditorium. They went backstage, where only a little light seeped through and everything was dark and gloomy. "You may be interested, my fine young friend, to know that this theater has a special trapdoor right here at the back of the stage. It leads down into a small pit that is quite soundproof, so you will be unable to hear the performance tomorrow night. A pity. But then no one in the audience will be able to hear your screams!" The creature stooped and slipped a finger into what looked like a knothole in the wood. Then with a tug it lifted the trapdoor. "Enjoy your brief stay!" cried Vanderhelm's voice, and Lewis yelped as he tumbled down.

He hit hard, with a jolt that left him breathless. His chest heaving, he scrambled to his feet. Two feet overhead, the oblong of dim light narrowed as the trapdoor swung downward. Lewis gasped a long breath and frantically tore at his muffler. He threw one end of it up just as the door was about to shut. Lewis tugged. The muffler was caught. Part of it must be sticking out of the trapdoor—would Vanderhelm see it?

After a long minute, Lewis concluded that he hadn't. But what good would it do him, unless someone came looking? Someone like Rose Rita or Mrs. Jaeger. That was exactly what Lewis was hoping for. It was the kind of wish that Mrs. Zimmermann always called a forlorn hope. Now he knew what she meant by that.

The air was close and musty, the darkness complete. Lewis felt around. He seemed to be in a kind of well with rough brick walls. It was about four feet square and maybe seven feet deep. He shuffled around and caught his foot in something that made a dull clatter.

Lewis stooped carefully and fumbled in the corner, feeling for whatever had snagged his foot. Something rattled under his touch, like fragments of broken porcelain. His fingers ran over curved shapes, smooth and cool to the touch, and something that was like a hard round ball. Then he felt the teeth.

Lewis screamed in terror. Now he knew where the ghost had come from. He had found the final resting place of poor Mordecai Finster.

# CHAPTER THIRTEEN

When Rose Rita gasped out the story of what had happened at the theater, Mrs. Jaeger looked as if she were going to faint. "Oh, dear," she murmured. "This is terrible!"

"What can we do?" asked Rose Rita. They were sitting in Mrs. Jaeger's kitchen, drinking mugs of hot cocoa. It was almost eleven o'clock on a dark night with no moon but lots of stars. It was well past her bedtime, but Rose Rita was afraid to go home. Afraid because her mother, under the evil spell of that dreadful man, might accidentally lead Mr. Vanderhelm to her. The wicked musician surely realized that Rose Rita had been the other person in the theater with Lewis, and heaven knew what he would do if he got his hands on her. Heaven knew what he might already have done to Lewis, for that matter. "Help me think, Mrs. Jaeger. We've got to do something," pleaded Rose Rita.

"Of course we do," replied Mrs. Jaeger with a nervous frown. "Let me see. First, we can't call the police, because we know some of the policemen are actually in that opera and under Vanderhelm's spell. Second, we can't go to the theater tonight, because Mr. Vanderhelm, or whoever that horror is, would be on his guard. It's almost the witching hour too, when evil things are strongest, and you already know how weak I am at magic. Well, since Mr. Vanderhelm never detected my presence, I suppose we're safe enough here. At least he hasn't tried to make me and my house vanish, and my feeling is that he simply doesn't know about me. However, it won't do just to sit here and be idle. I know what I wish we could do—"

Rose Rita grunted in irritation. She was used to Mrs. Zimmermann, who made up her mind quickly and acted right away. Mrs. Jaeger's methodical plodding irritated Rose Rita, who preferred quick action. "What is that?" she asked.

Mrs. Jaeger gave her an apologetic smile. "Well, I wish we could go to Jonathan Barnavelt's house. You see, since Vanderhelm did not cast his spell over Jonathan's house, he will be unable to touch it."

"Why?" asked Rose Rita. By now she had talked with Mrs. Jaeger enough to know that while the old woman could perform very little magic, she knew a great deal about the subject.

Mrs. Jaeger took a moment or two to consider before

she responded. "It's complicated, but think of a magic spell as a work of art. Like, oh, a sculpture that is carved from stone. Once the sculpture is complete, it is complete. You can't take any more stone away without spoiling what you have. A spell is the same way. It is carved, so to speak, from the magic that exists inside and around the magician. Once it is complete, it can't be changed, except to be removed entirely. So if Vanderhelm tried to cast a spell to make Jonathan Barnavelt's house vanish, he might succeed, but then the houses of all the other magicians in New Zebedee would appear. Unless he did something very foolish, the magicians would return with the houses. I don't think Mr. Vanderhelm would care to face them."

"So we would be safe in Lewis's house?" asked Rose Rita.

Mrs. Jaeger looked worried. "I'm not sure we'd be safe anyplace. But I would feel better there than anywhere else, and there is always the possibility that the mirror in the hall could let us communicate with Jonathan or Florence. We'd have to be there for the spell to work, though."

"I forgot about the mirror," confessed Rose Rita. She wondered whether she should tell Mrs. Jaeger about the magic mirror that Mrs. Zimmermann had once owned. That one had caused Mrs. Zimmermann and Rose Rita to travel into the past and face a terrible sorcerer. But the story seemed too long to tell, so Rose Rita merely said, "Well, if Mrs. Holtz leaves early tomorrow, we could get in then. Lewis told me that she always locks the door, but I know where his uncle hides a spare key. What can we do tonight?"

"Get some sleep," replied Mrs. Jaeger. "We won't be any good to Lewis or anyone else if we worry ourselves sick. You may stay in the guest room tonight. One of my granddaughters' nightgowns will fit you, I think."

So Rose Rita went to bed unwillingly in Mrs. Jaeger's house, worrying about Lewis and wondering if anything they could do would stop the ghastly creature that called itself Vanderhelm.

As for Lewis, he had finally recovered control of himself. He had been terrified out of his wits for more than an hour. It was horrible to be locked in the dark with a skeleton, but there was nothing he could do to get away. Finally he calmed down a little. If only there were a gleam of light, he thought, it wouldn't be so bad. Just a thin beam, a candle's flame, would make him feel better. But he had no way of making a light, so standing in the dark, leaning against the rough brick wall, he tried to come up with something else.

An idea occurred to him. A terrible idea in a way, but it was all he could summon up. He tried two or three times to call a name out loud, but he lost his nerve each time. Finally, balling his trembling hands into fists and squeezing his eyes tightly shut, Lewis managed to squeak out a plaintive, "Mr. Finster?"

No answer. Lewis panted. His lungs wheezed as if there were no air in the little cubicle, but he could feel a faint breeze in the corner, where air came through the round holes in some of the bricks. What felt like suffocation was simply fear. He gathered all his nerve and said, "I call on the ghost of Mr. Mordecai Finster. I, uh, call upon it in the name of all that is good."

The temperature in the room suddenly dropped ten degrees. An icy chill ran down Lewis's spine. Someone was with him now. Someone or some *thing*. His hair bristled and goosebumps crinkled the skin of his arms.

"Stop him," wailed a low, soft voice, sounding lonely and tormented.

"I'm t-trying to," gasped Lewis. "Only M-Mr. Vanderhelm isn't r-real. He's m-made up of sheet music."

"It is a phantasm," the voice replied, its tone still eerie enough to freeze Lewis's blood. "The living Vanderhelm created a ghostly double of himself by a vile magical spell. In life I hid the enchanted music away, but you found it and thereby released the evil double of Vanderhelm upon the world. Now it will try to do its dead master's will and become the King of the Dead. Stop him, oh stop him!"

"C-could you n-not talk like that?" asked Lewis. "It's scaring me."

"Oh. Sorry," said the voice in more companionable tones. "Didn't mean to get on your nerves. One gets used to being a ghost, you know. My spirit has haunted this wretched theater ever since I died of cruel thirst and slow starvation after Vanderhelm locked me away in this dark hole."

Lewis found he could breathe again. Mr. Finster's voice had completely changed. Now he sounded a bit absentminded, but friendly and encouraging. It helped a little. "Why did you haunt the theater?" Lewis asked.

"To keep anyone from releasing the spell, of course," answered the voice. "Only you found it so quickly. I hadn't materialized in so long, I was a bit rusty. It took me too much time to become solid enough to be visible to mortal eyes or to make myself heard. I tried to warn you."

"I'm sorry," said Lewis.

"Ah, well, it couldn't be helped." The voice took on a melancholy tone: "I was hoping you could somehow destroy the music and the spell, you see. Then I would be free at last."

Lewis blinked in the darkness. "I don't understand."

"I am bound to earth by my determination to help rid the world of Vanderhelm's foul enchantments," explained the voice. "If the spell is broken, then I may depart. If the charm is fulfilled, however—" the voice dropped to a low, frightening whisper— "if it is fulfilled, then I will rise up and be enslaved by Vanderhelm's cursed will. I hope that does not happen, boy, for your sake."

"You w-wouldn't hurt me?" squeaked Lewis.

"Of course not," said the voice. "But when the opera is sung through, Vanderhelm's spell will be complete, and the dead will arise to do his bidding. And once that happens, the ban will be lifted."

"What b-ban?" asked Lewis.

"The ban against spilling blood," returned the voice. "That is why the original Vanderhelm did not kill me outright. To do so would have ruined his chances of completing his horrible spell. You see, I stole the dreadful music score from his dressing room and was hurrying out with it when I heard Vanderhelm coming up the stairs. I remembered he was planning to replace the piano in the orchestra pit, so I thrust the music inside the old one, hoping it would be carried out the very next day. Unfortunately, Vanderhelm caught me and could tell I was up to something. He tried to make me talk, but I refused. Finally he threw me in this dismal hole, and early the next morning my friend Lucius Mickleberry sealed Vanderhelm's fate, but alas! I was never found—never found!"

Lewis started to shake again. "W-what can I do?" he asked with a groan.

"Use whatever you can!" returned the ghost. "Use whatever I leave you! My time grows short. Farewell, Lewis Barnavelt! Who knocks may enter—or leave!"

The darkness grew a little warmer. Lewis called out Mr. Finster's name once or twice, but no one answered. Dazed and utterly confused by the ghost's parting words, Lewis huddled in a corner, as far away from the pile of bones as possible. Sheer exhaustion overtook him, and at last he slept.

# CHAPTER FOURTEEN

The next morning dawned gray and chilly. Rose Rita and Mrs. Jaeger waited until ten o'clock, the time the rehearsals had always taken place. Then they drove over to the Barnavelt house in Mrs. Jaeger's black 1939 Chevrolet. Rose Rita saw a light burning in the front upstairs bedroom that Mrs. Holtz used, and a moment later she saw Mrs. Holtz herself walk past the window. She and Mrs. Jaeger waited for a long time, but Mrs. Holtz did not come out. Finally, they drove back to Mrs. Jaeger's house, where Rose Rita used the telephone to call home.

"Rose Rita!" her mother said in a stern voice. "Where in the world have you been? I got home late last night and thought you were in your room, and then this morning I found your bed hadn't even been slept in!"

"Here, dear," said Mrs. Jaeger. She took the receiver

from a stricken Rose Rita and said sweetly into it, "Louise? Hello, this is Mildred Jaeger. Oh, fine, dear . . . yes, Rose Rita told me you were singing in the opera. Yes, I'm sure it's very exciting. Well, I wanted to tell you that I'm the reason Rose Rita wasn't home. She offered to help me with a few things around the house, and then last night we were playing Monopoly. I intended to drive her home when we finished the game, but we fell sound asleep. Yes, both of us. And we didn't wake up until this morning, so of course I had her call. I'm terribly sorry if we worried you . . . yes, certainly. I'll be delighted to bring her tonight. I hope it's a good show." She hung up and said, "Whew!"

"Thank you, Mrs. Jaeger," said Rose Rita in a small voice. She hated to deceive her mother, but what choice did she have? "What did Mom say about the show?"

"Well, there's no rehearsal today, because the performance will be tonight at seven. Everyone is supposed to report to the theater at four, she says, so I suppose we'll just have to wait until then."

"What about Lewis?" wailed Rose Rita. "That awful Mr. Vanderhelm has him!"

"I know, dear, and I'm sorry. I'm afraid there's nothing we can do until we have a chance at that mirror."

"B-but . . ." Rose Rita blinked. Behind her spectacles, her eyes felt hot and itchy. "But we h-have to do something."

With a sad smile, Mrs. Jaeger said, "Now, don't give up hope, Rose Rita. Remember what I told you. Lewis is safe, at least until the detestable opera is performed.

We'll just have to make our move at the right time and do everything we can to help him."

"But it's not *fair*!" insisted Rose Rita. "It wasn't even Lewis's idea that we go down into that orchestra pit last night. It was mine. If something happens to him, it's all my f-fault—" she broke off with a choking sob.

Mrs. Jaeger spread her arms wide. Rose Rita fell against her and cried hot tears of anger, frustration, and fear.

The hours of the dead, dull day trickled by with agonizing slowness. Rose Rita would look at the clock, spend what seemed a long time doing something else, and look back, only to find that no more than five minutes had passed. All day long she worried and fretted about Lewis. Usually he was the worrywart. Lewis had a real talent for dreaming up horrible things that might happen but never did. Now Rose Rita was the one imagining all sorts of terrors and working herself up into a state over them.

Mrs. Jaeger made grilled-cheese sandwiches and tomato soup for lunch, but neither of them ate very much. The day grew darker and cloudier, and an unearthly hush settled over everything. New Zebedee appeared to be holding its breath, anticipating some great and terrible event. Finally, at ten minutes to four, neither Mrs. Jaeger nor Rose Rita could stand the wait any longer. They climbed into the old black Chevrolet and drove over to High Street. They arrived just in time to see Mrs. Holtz bustling away in her black coat, her heavy purse swinging by her side.

At Rose Rita's suggestion, Mrs. Jaeger parked her car around back, just outside the garage where Jonathan Barnavelt's 1935 Muggins Simoon was housed. Rose Rita came around front, nervously looking left and right. No one was watching. The house number, 100, in red reflecting numerals, was bolted to the iron fence around the front yard. Rose Rita grasped the 1 and tugged. It pulled away from the fence, and she twisted it to the right. The numeral, which was about a quarter of an inch deep, was hollow, and the spare key was inside. Rose Rita turned the numeral back to its normal position and pushed until it clicked into place. Then she unlocked the door and she and Mrs. Jaeger went into the front hall.

"What time is it?" asked Rose Rita.

Mrs. Jaeger looked at her watch. "Nearly four-fifteen."

Rose Rita groaned. They had less than three hours before the performance began. What could they do, even if they managed to reach Jonathan or Mrs. Zimmermann? The two of them were far away in Florida. They could never return to Michigan in time to fight the evil spell. Still, Rose Rita knew they had to try. They stood in front of the hat stand, and wielding her wooden spoon, Mrs. Jaeger said firmly, "I know I am not a very accomplished magician, but there is good magic here. I call upon it to help us! Show us Jonathan Barnavelt or Florence Zimmermann now!"

Rose Rita bit her lip. The mirror reflected nothing but their two anxious faces. Then it shimmered again, filling with swirls of color. When it cleared, Rose Rita blinked in surprise. A chubby, red-bearded man in strange medieval garb was tinkering with what looked like a human head made of bronze or brass. He glanced toward them, jumped in his seat, and cried out, "By Saint Loy! What vision is this?"

"Sorry, Friar Bacon," called Mrs. Jaeger apologetically. "Carry on!" The vision faded. "I can never get these things right," muttered Mrs. Jaeger. "Now I suppose Roger Bacon was distracted at a crucial moment, and that's why his talking brass head would only chatter about the time. Let me try again." She repeated her spell, and once again the mirror shimmered. This time Rose Rita shouted out in joy.

She was looking into a familiar pair of kindly blue eyes behind gold-rimmed spectacles. Eyes that were crinkly and friendly and knowing. "Mrs. Zimmermann!" she shouted.

The eyes blinked. Then they looked away. A moment later Mrs. Zimmermann pulled her head back. Now Rose Rita could see her whole face. "Good heavens!" said Mrs. Zimmermann, in a perfectly clear though faint voice. "Rose Rita, you nearly frightened me into plowing Bessie right into a telephone pole!" She glanced to her right and said, "It's Rose Rita, that's who, Weird Beard. Can't you hear her? Well, I can, and I can see her in the rearview mirror too!"

Jonathan Barnavelt then leaned into view, his head close to Mrs. Zimmermann's. "Sure enough," he said, and this time Rose Rita could hear his voice. "Rose

Rita, what in the world is going on in New Zebedee? We tried to drive in, but we couldn't make it through the fog."

"You're here in New Zebedee?" asked Rose Rita, her heart soaring.

"Close to it," said Mrs. Zimmermann. "Actually, we are driving away from you, toward my cottage on Lyon Lake. Tell us what's happened."

Rose Rita and Mrs. Jaeger hastily told all about Mr. Vanderhelm and the opera. When Rose Rita explained how Lewis had been captured by the specter that had come from the sheets of music, Jonathan looked so stricken that Rose Rita thought he was going to burst into tears. Mrs. Zimmermann's face set into a hard mask of determination. When at last the story ended, she said very distinctly, "Rose Rita, you had better take Mrs. Jaeger next door to my house. The key is under the doormat. You know the spare room where I keep all my amulets and talismans. You will have to look for a very special one. Now, pay close attention." She began to describe a magical amulet, a pearl with Hebrew letters scribed onto its surface. And then she told the two exactly what they had to do with it. "We'll be at the city limits at seven sharp," she finished. "If everything works, we have a chance. Go now, and hurry!"

When Mrs. Jaeger and Rose Rita went outside, it was only five o'clock, but the sky was already as dark as night. Gloom brooded over the whole countryside. As they hurried next door, Rose Rita hoped she could find what

Mrs. Zimmermann needed, and that they would not be too late to stop the evil spell and save Lewis's life.

Lewis was cold, hungry, and frightened. Mostly frightened. But he had been afraid for so long that he was almost used to it by now. He had spent an uncomfortable day trying to think of some way to escape from this horrible trap, but nothing had occurred to him. Mr. Finster's ghost had advised him to use what he had, but he didn't have very much. He wore his wristwatch, jacket, shirt, jeans, underwear, socks, and Keds. He also had the muffler that hung from the closed trapdoor. In his shirt pocket was a comb and his mechanical pencil. He carried a wallet in his jeans, but all it held were pictures of his mother and father and Uncle Jonathan and a single limp dollar bill. He couldn't see the use in any of these things.

He wished his watch at least had luminous numbers so that he could tell the time. He thought it might be very late, perhaps even time for the opera to start, but he had no way of judging. Then he heard something. A squeak. It came from above him.

"Hey!" he yelled, but his throat was so dry it came out as a croak. He heard the squeak again. Someone was walking on the trapdoor. He yelled again.

Then he remembered that Vanderhelm had said the trap was soundproof. No noise he made would be heard outside, unless he could pound against the trapdoor itself. What had the ghost said? *Who knocks may enter— or leave.* That was it. But the trapdoor was far over his head. He could not reach it.

And then a creepy thought came to Lewis. *Use whatever you have*, the ghost had advised, *whatever I leave you*. Well, nothing that Lewis had on him would help him. However, the ghost had left something else.

His skeleton.

Shivering and shaking, Lewis ran his hands over the hard, dry surface of the bones. He touched a long one, possibly an arm bone, and picked it up. He probed upward with it. Thunk! It was long enough to touch the trapdoor. He pounded with it, knocking so hard that the sound exploded in his tiny enclosed cell like gunshots. *Wham! Wham! Wham!*

He shoved hard and felt a slight movement. The trapdoor edged open about an inch or so, and he saw a dim crack of light, but that was as far as he could shove it.

"*Oof!*" Someone up above stumbled over the partly open door and grunted in surprise or pain. "What in the world—?"

Lewis heard someone scrabbling at the door. "Help!" he called. "I'm stuck in here."

The door opened up, and dim light trickled in as Lewis dropped the bone. A dark silhouette peered down toward him. "Who's there?" It was the voice of Mr. McGillis, one of the barbers in town. "It's too blamed dark t' see!"

"My muffler's stuck under the back edge of the door," Lewis said. "Hold onto it while I climb out."

Mr. McGillis was a big, beefy man. He grabbed the muffler and held it, while Lewis scrambled up as if he were climbing a rope. He dragged himself over the edge and scooted away from the trapdoor on all fours. Mr. McGillis let the door slam back into place. "Lewis Barnavelt, ain't it?" he said. "What in th' Sam Hill you doin' in there, Lewis?"

"You've got to help me," gasped Lewis. "I—"

A blare of horns and a rattle of drums sounded suddenly. "Sorry, kiddo," said Mr. McGillis. "Mr. Vanderhelm decided to begin the performance an hour early. Last act's startin', and I'm on. See ya later!" And he ducked between the curtains and was gone.

Lewis looked at his watch. It was almost seven o'clock. If the opera lasted an hour and a half, then all the dead would rise in only thirty-two minutes.

And the grisly creature that called itself Henry Vanderhelm would be the King of the Dead forever.

# CHAPTER FIFTEEN

Fog clung to Rose Rita's cheeks and arms and legs in a disgusting caress. She didn't even want to breathe, because she hated the thought of drawing that nasty stuff into her lungs. She and Mrs. Jaeger had taken a few steps into the thick mist. They had just crossed the railroad tracks and now stood in choking darkness, with the grayness curling and swirling around them, making ugly shapes a little denser than the night. Rose Rita held the amulet before her.

It was about the size of a marble, a smooth white globe with a few markings on it that were the Hebrew letters placed there in ancient times by a great magician who understood the Cabala, a mystical doctrine of powerful lore. Mrs. Zimmermann had given Mrs. Jaeger the spell to pronounce at the right moment, and an anxious Mrs.

Jaeger was going over and over the speech, whispering it just under her breath.

"It's time," Rose Rita said. "Mrs. Zimmermann said they'd prepare at her cottage and be here at seven o'clock. It's seven now, Mrs. Jaeger."

Taking a deep breath, Mrs. Jaeger began to recite a bizarre rhyme that included words from Basque, Finno-Ugric, and Tagalog as well as Hebrew, Latin, and Greek. It required her to cry out a short, sharp *yah!* at the end of every verse, which she did with gusto, only to murmur, "Oh, dear," before resuming the rest of the spell. At the same time, she waved her magic wooden spoon as if she were stirring a pot of bubbling oatmeal. At last the incantation ended with the word *lux* repeated emphatically three times. Rose Rita thought it was odd that a magic spell should end with the name of a dish detergent, but then magic was not her field.

When the last cry of *lux!* died away, something happened. Rose Rita noticed a tautening of the string on which the amulet dangled. She held on tightly.

And then the amulet began to bounce merrily up and down, like a yo-yo. "Uh, Mrs. Jaeger?" muttered Rose Rita. "I think you did something wrong. Why not try again, without the 'Oh-dears' this time?"

"I knew this would happen," sniffled Mrs. Jaeger. But she started over, and as soon as she began the chant, the amulet stopped its silly behavior. Mrs. Jaeger went all the way through, and at the last word, the pearly globe suddenly began to quiver on its string.

Rose Rita strained to see if it was doing anything.

With the darkness, the fog, and the menacing shapes that loomed up on all sides of her, it was hard to see anything. No, there it was: The little white ball was barely visible. Was it growing brighter? Rose Rita thought it might be, and she was just about to ask Mrs. Jaeger if she thought so, when—

*Whoosh!* With a sound like bursting flame, the amulet threw off a brilliant white illumination. The fog shrank back all around them. Rose Rita had to squint against the fierce light. She half turned her head. Mrs. Jaeger, who had thrown her arm up to shield her eyes, was all white highlights and black shadows, like an ink sketch of herself. Even looking away from the amulet, Rose Rita's eyes streamed tears. The magic charm was working! She could see the street below her feet, and a few yards of the rusty-red railroad track behind her. But was the amulet bright enough to penetrate to the other side of the fog? If it wasn't, they were lost.

"Listen!" said Mrs. Jaeger.

With her heart trying to climb into her mouth, Rose Rita listened. Something was approaching. A crunchy, crackling sound came from in front of them, as if something very large were drawing near. Something like a hungry dinosaur, perhaps, or a stalking tiger, or a stealthy grizzly bear, or—

"A car!" shouted Mrs. Jaeger. "I see the headlights."

"Bessie!" Rose Rita yelled at the same moment. The dim headlights, small as two dimes, crept closer and closer. Rose Rita took a slow step back, and then another, across the railroad tracks. She edged out of the fog, and the headlights still followed the unearthly gleam of the amulet. At last the purple nose of Mrs. Zimmermann's beloved Bessie broke through the clinging fog, and a second later Mrs. Zimmermann and Jonathan Barnavelt spilled out of the two front doors of the car. Its work done, the amulet faded as Rose Rita rushed into Mrs. Zimmermann's arms. "Lewis," gasped Rose Rita. "We have to save him."

"That's why we're here," growled Jonathan. "Mildred, you really came through with the goods this time! Now pile into the car everyone. We've got to get to the opera house."

Mrs. Zimmermann waited until they were all inside, and then she put Bessie in gear. They sped through the deserted streets, turned onto Main, and pulled up in front of the opera house. As Jonathan opened his door, a faint sound of music and singing filtered into the car. He gave Mrs. Zimmermann a worried glance. "Sounds like the fun's already started, Florence," he said in a low voice.

"Then we have to finish it," Mrs. Zimmermann returned. "Everybody out! Mildred, do you remember the Words of Banishing Evil?"

"Of course, Florence," said Mrs. Jaeger. "But I'm so awfully bad at saying them—"

"You won't be saying them alone," said Mrs. Zimmermann. "Jonathan and I will be repeating them too. And one of us *has* to finish the spell, no matter what happens to the others. Just remember that!" She grasped her umbrella firmly and opened her door. "Rose Rita, I suppose it's no use telling you to stay in the car, so you can come along. But don't get too close. A wizard's duel can be a dangerous affair, and the farther you are from us old fogies, the better off you'll be. Now come along!"

Jonathan was already rattling the handle of the theater door. "Locked," he muttered. "I should have suspected that. Well, let me see if I can kick—"

"Oh, move aside, Brush Mush," said Mrs. Zimmermann in a brisk voice. She murmured something, and a sizzling purple ray shot out from the crystal orb that was held in place by a bronze griffin's talon on her umbrella. As the light grazed it, the whole doorknob glowed for a moment with purple light. "Try it now," she said.

Jonathan tugged, and the door opened. "Good going, Prunella," he said. "Now, let's—"

He broke off as something rushed out. It grabbed him and clung to him. "Oh!" shrieked Mrs. Zimmermann, and Mrs. Jaeger cried out in alarm.

But Rose Rita was laughing with relief.

The form that had hurtled out of the dark doorway was Lewis. He was alive, and he was all right.

It took him just a few moments to pant out the shocking story of his imprisonment. Jonathan snarled with anger when Lewis had finished. "That's it," he said. "By George, I may be a second-rate magician, but nobody is going to push my nephew around like that. Ready, troops? Let's show that infernal scarecrow that we mean business!"

Lewis dropped to the rear of the procession, beside Rose Rita. "Did you really talk to a ghost?" she whispered as they climbed the stairs.

"Yeah," Lewis said. "And he scared me at first, but then he tried to help me. And I got out of that gruesome little tomb by using one of his bones."

Lewis felt the claustrophobic Rose Rita shudder. "I would have gone out of my mind," she whispered.

They got to the top of the stairway. Like a general directing his army, Jonathan waved Mrs. Zimmermann over to the left archway. He whispered to Mrs. Jaeger, "Count to fifteen after I go in, and then follow me. But keep your distance." To Lewis and Rose Rita, he said, "You kids had better stay out here, or at least at the back of the theater. Don't believe anything you see. Whatever that fiend summons up might hurt a magician, but to anyone else it will all be moonshine and magic, and if you don't believe in it, it won't hurt you."

"This way," whispered Rose Rita. She grabbed Lewis's hand and tugged him toward the left archway, where Mrs. Zimmermann had vanished. Lewis gulped, but he followed her, step after reluctant step.

When they stood in the archway, he blinked. Mrs. Zimmermann stood transformed. Instead of her purple cloth coat and plain black umbrella, she wore billowing robes of purple, with red flames blazing in their folds, and she carried before her a tall ebony staff crowned with a blinding purple star. She was halfway down the aisle toward the stage, and she stalked forward, an imposing and fiery figure.

Vanderhelm stood at center stage, directing the large cast that surrounded him. His eyes flashed when he saw Mrs. Zimmermann, and his gestures quickened. The hapless actors began to sing faster, faster, breathing hard between the lines. Mrs. Zimmermann started to chant something, but the singing grew louder. A black winged form, an enormous bat, dropped down from the ceiling above. Its hideous mouth curled back from inch-long, needle-sharp fangs, and its slitted eyes glowed red as burning coals. Mrs. Zimmermann saw the plummeting monster and pointed her staff. The grimacing bat silently exploded in a purple blaze a yard above Mrs. Zimmermann's head, but she staggered, and Vanderhelm's eyes flashed in victory.

Then Jonathan Barnavelt's deep voice boomed out in the same chant. The singers faltered and their voices weakened. For a moment Lewis dared hope that his uncle was winning.

But then Vanderhelm began to sing, in a cruel, commanding baritone. Behind Jonathan a theater seat ripped itself loose and began to walk on its four cast-iron legs. It swelled and changed shape as it came up behind Jonathan, until it was a four-legged monstrosity with its arms ending in wicked, sharp claws. The seat grew long and suddenly split into a gaping, drooling mouth, all pointed teeth and lashing forked tongue. Jonathan sensed it as it crouched to spring on him. He whirled, pointed his cane, and yelled one word, sharp and cold as steel. The monster flew backward as if struck by a car, and when it landed halfway up the aisle, it was just a seat again. But Vanderhelm had succeeded in breaking Jonathan's spell, and one more competing voice was stilled. Lewis saw his uncle reach for his throat as he stumbled backward, croaking hoarse, horrible sounds.

"This is the last aria!" Rose Rita cried. "When he finishes it, the dead will rise!"

Mrs. Jaeger had moved to the middle of the back row. She timidly began to chant, waving her wooden spoon in rhythm to the words, but with a single gesture Vanderhelm froze the words in her throat. She almost fell backward into one of the theater seats.

His voice rising, swelling, Vanderhelm sang still louder, leering in hideous triumph. Mrs. Zimmermann was waving her wand, but her other hand clutched at her throat. Lewis wanted to turn and run away.

Instead he shouted to Rose Rita, "We know the score! We're the ones who can stop him! It's what the magician in the mirror told us!" He ran toward the stage, and Rose Rita ran beside him. They passed Mrs. Zimmermann, one on each side, in a bread-and-butter split, and they were abreast again. "Call this opera?" bellowed Lewis at the top of his lungs. "Boy, you stink!"

Vanderhelm blinked at him, but he continued to sing, a hateful snarl writhing on his lips. "Lewis!" screamed Rose Rita. "What are you doing?"

"No wonder old Vanderflop started the show without an audience," Lewis screamed back at her. " 'Cause he knew they'd boo him. What a ham!"

Rose Rita caught on. "You're flat!" she screeched.

"You're so far off-key, you couldn't find it with both hands! You couldn't carry a tune in a milk bucket! P.U., you stink! Where'd you learn to sing—in a monkey house?"

"Yah, yah, yah!" roared Lewis. "You sound like a moose with a bellyache!"

"And the tune is awful," put in Rose Rita. "My grandpa could write better music, and he's tone-deaf!"

"What is it—'Concerto for Goofballs?'" heckled Lewis. "You can't write for sour apples, Vanderstupid!"

"*How dare you!*" Vanderhelm did not sing the words. He bellowed them at the top of his lungs, and the confused orchestra blatted to a ragged pause. "*How dare you mock the greatest creation of—*"

"Now!" yelled Jonathan, and all three magicians—he, Mrs. Jaeger, and Mrs. Zimmermann—chanted out something hot and angry and powerful. Their booming voices swelled and filled the auditorium. Lewis sensed the mounting power, like a huge wave about to break on a rocky shore.

Vanderhelm gasped and tried to sing again, but a mighty wind rose outside the theater, sounding as if it would rip the roof off. *Blam! Blam!* The doorway outside blasted open with a thunderclap, nearly torn off its hinges. *Crash!* The wind rushed into the auditorium, jangling the crystal of the great chandelier overhead. *Flap!* The curtains billowed, the sets teetered! With frightened yelps, the cast rushed offstage as the painted backdrops danced a crazy gavotte in the screeching wind.

*"No!"* screamed Vanderhelm. His eyes blazed at the musicians in the pit, and he shook his fist at them. *"Play, curse you, play!"*

But the magicians had scrambled up out of the orchestra pit and dashed out past Lewis and Rose Rita. The wind dipped down into the pit, fingering the strings of the violins, drawing shivery cat-screeches from the viola, puffing oompahs into the tuba, even thumping a funeral-march beat on the bass drum. And from the pit rose a cyclone of loose music sheets. They descended on a swaying Vanderhelm, whose faltering voice was trying vainly to hit a few final notes.

With a riffle like a giant deck of cards being shuffled, the figure of Vanderhelm dissolved into paper and ink, merging with the sheets of music flying through the air. Then, like an enormous snake the music-gorged wind swept in a sinuous curve out over everyone's heads, through the archway, down the stairs, and out into the night. A backdrop collapsed with a slap. Down in the orchestra pit a last, lingering breeze tinkled the triangle.

Lewis had a vision in his mind. Somehow he knew that the dead who lay in their graves in Oakridge Cemetery had been nearly stirred to life and to slavery, but all had just now lain back with sighs of relief. Somewhere a hideous stone statue had just now shattered. And in the brick pit beneath the stage, a pile of old bones, clattered to animation by the doomsday music, had now sunk wearily and gratefully to its rest.

A moment later heads peeked around the edges of the proscenium. Actors came shuffling back onto the stage amid the ruined set. They looked at each other with wide eyes, as if they had all just awakened from a sleep as deep as a woodchuck's winter hibernation. "Land sakes," said Mrs. Feeney, pointing at Mr. McGillis. "Mike, you're a sight!"

"What in thunder are we doing up here?" someone asked.

"I don't remember a thing," said someone else.

"Rose Rita? Rose Rita, is that you?" asked Mrs. Pottinger, shading her eyes. She was wearing a beaded gown and a high silver wig, and she didn't look anything like herself. But when Rose Rita rushed into her arms, her laugh was her old familiar laugh. "My stars!" she said. "I don't know what's going on, but whatever it is, I feel like a fool!"

"It's broken," Jonathan said, his hand on Lewis's shoulder. "The evil that started all those years ago. We did it, all of us. We've finally seen the last of old Vanderhelm."

# CHAPTER SIXTEEN

The following Saturday afternoon, Rose Rita, Mrs. Jaeger, and Mrs. Zimmermann all came to visit Jonathan and Lewis in the mansion on High Street. They had milk and some of Mrs. Zimmermann's wonderful walnut-fudge cookies, and they sat on lawn furniture in the backyard, because the weather had turned sunny and warm. The grass was beginning to show hints of green, and fresh buds had popped out on all the trees. The air held a wonderful scent of growing things. Spring had arrived at last.

"Well," said Jonathan as he finished his milk, "I suppose I had better start. First, you will be happy to hear that the Capharnaum County Magicians Society has all returned from Goony-Goony Land, or wherever it was that Vanderhelm sent them. I've talked to everyone in the society, and the story is always the same. Each one was trapped in his or her house by that horrible fog, just the way New Zebedee was trapped."

"But they're all magicians. Couldn't any of them use a spell to escape?" asked Rose Rita.

"No," answered Mrs. Zimmermann. "Because years ago old Vanderhelm worked out a particularly potent enchantment. You see, sometimes a magician can counter a spell that another magician has cast, but that requires both power and knowledge. One thing you have to know to fight a spell is just who cast it. And everyone in the society believed that Vanderhelm had died years ago, so they never even thought of him as the one responsible."

Lewis, who felt recovered from his series of frights, said, "I thought Vanderhelm *had* died a long time ago. I thought he perished in a magical duel with Lucius Mickleberry."

Jonathan made a wry face. "That's what we all believed, Lewis. Unfortunately, it was only partly true. As it turns out, Vanderhelm locked something of himself—namely, his insane wish to be King of the Dead—in a spell that brought to life a phantom duplicate of himself. A duplicate made up of the music that carried the spell. That creature was what you were up against."

Mrs. Zimmermann smiled at Lewis. "And in case you were wondering if you were responsible for bringing the monster to life, Lewis, the answer is a big, fat no. You see, when a wizard expires, all his active spells are broken. Lucius Mickleberry must have placed some kind of spell on Vanderhelm, maybe even after the wizard's duel was over. Perhaps he suspected that old Yowl-and-Howl had left behind some nasty little surprise. If the spell placed on the sheet music had been complete when the real Vanderhelm died, you see, it could not have been broken. But Lucius's protective spell would have kept the duplicate from coming to life, at least until Lucius himself passed away."

"Well," sighed Mrs. Jaeger, "at least all this uproar is over. Even though people from the outside world are laughing at New Zebedee for getting lost in a spring fog, everything turned out all right."

"Not everyone is laughing," Rose Rita said. "Ever since my uncle drove him back into town, Grandpa Galway has been pretty suspicious of what's been going on. He swears there's more to the story than anyone will tell him. It's funny how no one remembers anything about the opera."

"Not so funny at all, Rose Rita," answered Jonathan. "Magic has a way of doing that. The main thing is that no one associated with that ridiculous opera can remember a single line of the music. That means Vanderhelm's spell is broken forever. To tell you the truth, I think all the actors and musicians feel foolish about the whole thing. Miss White at the school is putting it all down to some bizarre form of spring fever. It's best to let the good folks of New Zebedee think they just went a little goofy after a long, hard winter, so we'll leave it at that."

Mrs. Jaeger nodded and said, "I suppose the old theater will be sealed up."

"Nonsense," said Mrs. Zimmermann in her brisk voice. "The curse is lifted, just as the fog around the town has lifted. And with the bones of poor Mordecai Finster decently laid to rest in Oakridge Cemetery, no ghost will haunt the opera house from now on. The theater will be absolutely harmless. In fact, I am going to suggest at the next meeting of the board of education that the auditorium be turned over to the school. They have needed a place for pageants and plays for years, and it would fit the bill perfectly."

Lewis sighed. "I was petrified of Mr. Finster's ghost," he admitted. "But he only wanted to help me. I hope his spirit is at rest now."

"I think so, Lewis," said his uncle. "A ghost can rest when its purpose has been fulfilled on earth. And just to make sure that nothing like that will ever happen again, some friends of mine and I went over and filled poor Mordecai's cell with cement."

"At any rate," said Mrs. Jaeger, "it is all finished. I'm happy I could help in a small way."

Jonathan's deep laughter boomed through the yard. " 'Small way?' Well, I'll admit that Lewis and Rose Rita made Vanderhelm's defeat possible when they became music critics. Hitting that nasty creature right in his vanity worked like a charm and let us counteract his magic. Still, Mildred, you were the hero of the hour! Shall we tell her, Frizzy Wig?"

Mrs. Zimmermann's eyes sparkled with mischief. "I suppose so, Fuzzy Mug. After all, the meeting is to-night."

With a broad smile Jonathan said, "Mildred, to be elected to membership in the Capharnaum County Magicians Society, you have to prove yourself by working out a real magic spell all by yourself. I got in by eclipsing the moon, and Pruny Face here by—well, that's another story. Anyway, your success with the mirror and light spells demonstrates that you qualify. I've talked to all the other magicians, and they've agreed. Congratulations. You are the newest member of the Capharnaum County Magicians Society."

Mrs. Jaeger's hands flew to her cheeks. She blushed with pleasure and embarrassment. "Oh, dear," she said. "I don't know what to say!"

"Don't say anything, Mildred," Mrs. Zimmermann told her. "Just come to the meeting tonight. We'll have the formal ceremony then."

"I've never been to a meeting like that before. Oh, dear, what shall I wear?" Mrs. Jaeger asked.

Jonathan smiled. "Oh, anything you wish," he said. "Be casual, be comfortable, and be yourself. But one thing—" he broke off, his eyes growing round with alarm. "What's that?"

Lewis's heart thudded. A piping, eerie music filled the air, a haunting, faraway tune that was growing louder by the second. Everyone leaped up and stared at the corner of the house.

A second later Jailbird the cat sauntered around the house and into the backyard. He was whistling "Buffalo Gals" so badly it sounded like a funeral dirge.

Mrs. Jaeger looked pained. "At least," she said, "I'm

not as terrible a magician as whoever enchanted that poor cat!"

Mrs. Zimmermann began to laugh. Uncle Jonathan turned a bright pink, but then he chuckled too. Looking pleased with himself, Jailbird finished his tune and began to wash his paws as Mrs. Jaeger, Rose Rita, and Lewis joined in the laughter. It was a good sound, a lively sound, in the warm sunshine of the first real day of spring.

# JOHN BELLAIRS

is the critically acclaimed, best-selling author of many Gothic novels, including *The Drum, the Doll, and the Zombie; The Lamp from the Warlock's Tomb; The Mansion in the Mist; The Curse of the Blue Figurine; The Mummy, the Will, and the Crypt; The Spell of the Sorcerer's Skull; The Revenge of the Wizard's Ghost; The Chessmen of Doom; The Eyes of the Killer Robot;* and the previous novels starring Lewis Barnavelt and Rose Rita Pottinger, *The House with a Clock in Its Walls; The Figure in the Shadows; The Letter, the Witch, and the Ring; The Ghost in the Mirror;* and *The Vengeance of the Witch-Finder.*

John Bellairs died in 1991. Brad Strickland, a longtime Bellairs fan, has completed *The Doom of the Haunted Opera,* just as he did *The Ghost in the Mirror; The Vengeance of the Witch-Finder;* and *The Drum, the Doll, and the Zombie.*